Translated by Türker Çiftçi

Published by Blue Dome Press
335 Clifton Avenue, Clifton
New Jersey 07011, USA

www.bluedomepress.com

Library of Congress Cataloging-in-Publication Data

Names: Alpgüvenç, Can, 1945- author. | Çiftçi, Türker, translator.
Title: Death of the Pharaoh / Can Alpgüvenç ; [translated by Türker Çiftçi].
Other titles: Firavun'un Ölümü. English
Description: Clifton, New Jersey : Blue Dome Press, 2016.
Identifiers: LCCN 2015046569 | ISBN 9781935295877 (alk. paper)
Subjects: LCSH: Egypt--History--To 332 B.C.--Fiction. | Moses (Biblical leader)--Fiction.
Classification: LCC PL248.A515 F5813 2016 | DDC 894/.3534--dc23
LC record available at http://lccn.loc.gov/2015046569

Printed by
Çağlayan A.Ş., Izmir - Turkey

DEATH OF
THE PHARAOH

Can Alpgüvenç

NEW JERSEY • LONDON • FRANKFURT • CAIRO

BLUE DOME

The Strings of Your Instrument Are Attached to My Heart

*I*t was midday. Everything was asleep under the sun, which was wildly scorching the vicinity. Shadows had shortened to almost a line. There wasn't the slightest movement in the palm tree leaves that could be seen from behind the garden walls. In the streets of Thebes which resembled a ghost town, nobody but black slaves could be seen. These huge men with nothing but a striped cloth they wore beneath their waist were carrying water from the Nile in the water jugs on their shoulders.

Sorrowful melodies were spreading from the garden of the palace far away. The garden was skirted by big trees. In the middle, a somewhat large pool with lotus flowers floating in it, and behind it a small and elegant mansion could be seen. The walls were painted faint pink and were decorated with flower patterns.

A young girl whose face and body had fine lines and was extraordinarily beautiful was sitting in one of the gilded armchairs in the lounge. This girl was dressed in a manner peculiar only to youth of the palaces of Thebes.

This beautiful princess with an embroidered cover on her lap was looking around absentmindedly. With a cover on her lap, Tiye was leaning on one side of the armchair and listening to the song without moving at all. The stillness of her body was interrupted every now and then by her sighing deeply.

* * *

When the brown haired girl stopped upon the sign of the beautiful princess who had shed a few tears, the lounge lapsed into silence all of a sudden.

"It is as if the strings of your instrument are attached to my heart. Their vibration hurts my heart, your songs make my wounds bleed."

"My dear princess, the gods have given the keys to secret feelings to composers. They interpret feelings that can't be expressed by words. If my song upsets you I can play an entertaining song."

She slowly shook her head; her lips were sealed. Taking courage from being her maid, Tesi said:

"What is there to be so sad about? You're young, and beautiful enough to make beautiful women jealous. You live as you wish in this wonderful mansion given to you by your father Haman. You have the most beautiful garden in Egypt. In your trunk decorated with diamonds you have priceless jewels, gold bracelets, ear rings, pearl and coral necklaces. The number of your clothes isn't even known. Why are you so troubled, when your heart should open in joy like an elegant lotus flower?"

"You don't understand me Tesi. There is no doubt that the gods have been very gracious to me, but what use is it if my heart doesn't get what it wants? Despite my gilded mansion, my gardens decorated by lotuses, and trunks full of jewels, I am more miserable than those black colored slaves that carry water from the Nile in water jugs on their shoulders."

"But princess, if what you want can't be found in Egypt isn't it brought to your feet with the caravans of Korah from lands far away?"

Tiye smiled bitterly and shook her head hopelessly. Meanwhile Tesi had understood how meaningless her words were and stopped talking. However, a little later she broke the silence again:

"Are you thinking about the young prince you saw last year at the festival of god Min?"

"..."

"He looked so handsome in his academy uniform."

"It is said that school holidays are about to start, I think you will be reunited soon."

A slight pinkness spread over Tiye's face. Tesi was determined to continue with her consolation speech that she had started:

"Your sorrows will end my beautiful princess."

"This morning I was strolling in the garden. The sun was just rising. I was startled by the sound of the flowers. They were looking at me with pity, whispering among themselves: O gloomy girl, how lovely the sun warms your cheeks, but cold winter rules over your heart."

"O my emotional princess."

"I had a dream last night. In the dark of the night I was walking in a magical garden with Sinuha. Birds were chirping, the quivering moonlight was softly illuminating everywhere. As I was looking at him with love, he had knelt, but all of a sudden a black and ugly giant came between us. Scared, I moved back; the prince was drenched in blood. I shouted so much that the giant retreated in confusion, he vanished in the weary light."

"Don't think ill of it madam."

The warm tears that were running from Tiye's green eyes had started to roll down her cheeks.

"Tesi, do you know who the ugly giant in my dream was?"

"Who was it madam?"

"It was my father. He never liked Sinuha, and he never will. I'm afraid of him doing evil."

"Dreams are the wrong way around princess."

After taking a deep breath the princess said:

"Your songs are venomous Tesi, venomous. Start to vibrate the strings of your harp, kill me slowly with the painful sorrow of your melodies. Come on, destroy my heart with your magical plucking."

As the brown haired maid moved her fingers over the strings of the harp, sorrow covered the lounge once again.

* * *

A black slave with a sweaty body that was only covered beneath the waist with a striped cloth entered all of a sudden, bowed respectfully and said:

"Your father is here madam."

The harp had stopped. Tesi ran out of the lounge like a shadow. Tiye put a fake smile on her face. Grand Vizier Haman and his wife had already entered the lounge. Haman was a tall, heavy-built, and strong man. He always looked angry. He couldn't be considered ugly, there weren't any annoying elements on his face, other than his bulging eyes. The thing that really made him ugly was his heart full of cruelty and hatred. Setting his bulging eyes on his one and only possession, he tried to smile. Then he turned to his wife and said:

"See Nitocris. My beautiful daughter is very happy in her magnificent palace with gardens watered by the Holy Nile. The god of beauty gave all the elegance in the universe to our Tiye."

Despite the fake smile on her face, Tiye was cold. Her father was diving deep into her looks, trying to explore her heart. Softening his harsh voice as much as he could:

"My dear daughter, our gods' representative on earth, the invincible Pharaoh will be in Thebes in a few days. Our conqueror of Nubia is returning with tens of thousands of black slaves and trunks full of jewels. There is the Egyptian Army with hundreds of chariots, thousands of cavalry and infantry behind him. I am going to welcome him with an appropriate ceremony. That day everyone in Thebes will gather in the shade of the great shrine of Amun. Don't you hear the horns? The festival has started already. You should prepare too, and take your place in your lodge in the stand when the time comes."

Tiye turned pale. She tried to hide the unhappy look on her face, but her disturbance hadn't escaped her father's eyes:

"My dear daughter, you know that following the great festival you will be married to the handsome chief commander Ubiante. He too will soon enter the city in the shade of the immortal Pharaoh with great pride. You should do all that you can to impress him."

From what jabbed her heart, Tiye's green eyes squinted in pain. Even though she wanted to cry out that she didn't love him, she didn't say anything at all.

The young commander was a soldier who was tall, had wide shoulders, and a nice face.

Haman had read it all in his daughter's eyes. After flashing a threatening look at her, he turned around. Her mother was cross with her too, she hadn't hugged her, and hadn't even talked to her. She had said a lot to try to make her give up on Sinuha. However, she couldn't convince Tiye. It wasn't that she didn't understand her daughter, but Haman would always have the last say. She knew how useless it was to resist him. When he reached the big pool where lotus flowers floated, Haman stopped all of a sudden, he met his wife's eyes:

"She still has Imhotep's son on her mind", he yelled.

"Darling, I spoke with her many times, I tried everything. But she loves him, I don't know what to do."

The Grand Vizier kicked the seat next to the pool with great rage, and it fell into the water. The fancy fish that were gliding in the water in harmony fled in fear. The surface of the pool was covered with crushed lotuses,

"She will forget Sinuha" he roared.

He looked angrily at his wife:

"She will marry Ubiante. Or else..."

His voice was so horrendous that even the black slaves in the garden crouched in fear on the very spot.

Tiye had seen what happened from the big window of the lounge. The tulle curtain was hiding her.

"I love him", she groaned.

One of the Children of Israel
Will Destroy the Pharaoh

They were sitting under trees, on a hill away from the wind; they were watching the sun rise, and it was illuminating the Nile which looked like it had swallowed the whole plain. The sun that was rising from behind the mountains very far in the east had quickly overcome the Nile and had lit up the Oleander Shrub District. The delta was preparing for a bright and brand new day.

Prince Sepi, the only son of the King of Amurru, cried out in joy:

"What a magnificent view."

The prince was studying politics in Memphis, one of the most developed cities of Lower Egypt. In the last week at the academy, he had joined the Faiyum Dam trip accompanied by Amun priests.

The empire was the only ruler of the region, and had left their internal affairs to many chiefdoms like Syria, Palestine and Byblos. Egypt would meddle in every case between chiefdoms and kingdoms, and would usually take on a judge's role, showing that they were dominant.

The sons of kings and chiefs in these countries would study in academies in Egypt, be raised with Egyptian culture and civilization, and when they came into power in their countries, they would be loyal slaves to Egypt. Egypt would also establish armies in countries bonded to them, and make use of them when necessary. Tax from the mentioned countries was one of the most important income sources of the empire.

Sinuha squinted proudly, and smiled. His smile had spread all over his face.

"It isn't easy for a foreigner to understand Egypt's power in a short span of time. There is a huge civilization hidden in our land from Elephantine to Avaris."

Sepi hadn't heard these words. He was looking at the wonderful view which was growing even more magnificent as the sun reflected its rays off the water, as if he was mesmerized.

All of a sudden he said:

"How did you restrain this uncontrollable torrent? How did you trap it into this huge pool? These high walls, impassable barriers, they are, they are unbelievable, unbelievable."

* * *

Sinuha's mother was a Phoenician concubine. She was enslaved by Egyptian sailors in a naval war offshore of Avaris, and when spoils were being shared, she was given as a concubine to the palace of Imhotep, the Agriculture Minister and brother of the Pharaoh.

Imhotep loved that golden haired, blue eyed girl so much that he first set her free, and then married her. Young Sinuha was an exact copy of his mother. He was very handsome with blond hair that fell on his shoulders, his round and white face, and his Nile blue eyes.

With an attitude of despising Prince Sepi, he said:

"A long time ago, when the Nile would swell, the whole valley would flood just like a sea, shrines and palaces would be encircled by waves. Then our ancestors started to think about a solution to prevent the Nile from madly overflowing. Finally, twenty centuries ago Pharaoh Amenemhat III managed to build a big dam in Memphis, next to the academy. To prevent his people from suffering from the overflowing and to develop agriculture in his land, that king transformed this swamp that you can see in Faiyum Oasis in to a dam. And now, all the water demand of Middle and Lower Egypt is supplied from this endless lake we are looking at. Our engineers flow the Nile's extra water through a wide canal to this lake. Both sides of the canal all the way to the Nile are decorated with statues of Pharaoh Amenemhat. Egypt doesn't fail to pay due respect to those who served their country."

"I'm very surprised."

"Egypt's power isn't limited to this. You must see the shrine made for Ra, in Abusir. It is decorated with such lifelike statues that you would be astonished."

Sepi was both listening to his friend and watching the wonderful view in front of him. Sinuha carried on:

"We are now experiencing the most powerful era of our history. My uncle, Ramesses II., both built hundreds of new shrines and renovated the old ones. For instance, the temple made by carving out rocks in Abu Simbel is an architectural masterpiece. From end to end, Egypt is a museum of civilization."

Sepi was disturbed by his friend over praising his country, and his face clouded over, he murmured:

"You despise us."

Sinuha lost his enthusiasm all of a sudden, he calmed down. He opened the collar studs of his red school cloak in a single movement, and hurled it towards the tree:

"Don't take offense now, I didn't tell you these things to upset you."

The tone of his voice had softened.

"To make true friends one should block an ear, and sometimes both of them. Listen Sepi, if the Nile gives us life, we owe it to these canal projects and dam reservoirs made by our ancestors. Egypt has been working for three thousand and five hundred years to accomplish this. You can only reach the pleasure of achievement through success, which is the result of hard work. You must see Pi

Ramesses which was built by my uncle. It is decorated with wonderful palaces and unique gardens. It is full of hundreds of god statues, each of them an art masterpiece. The large statues in our country increase our people's trust in their country. Thus, Egypt shows its strength to everyone, both friend and foe."

Sepi was continuing to listen silently. With a warm smile Sinuha said:

"Don't worry, I am your friend, and I always will be your friend. The truth shouldn't upset one. Success cannot be achieved without effort. Success first of all starts with believing; he who abandons hope loses before even starting."

Sepi felt a little relieved:

"It is not the truth, but your sarcastic attitude that upsets me."

"I didn't mean to hurt you."

The Amurru prince wanted to ask something, but was hesitating. With all his cheer Sinuha said:

"Come on, ask your question."

"Is it true that you ruthlessly work prisoners, slaves, and the Israelites under your ruling in the mines in Sinai and the stone quarries in Hamammet?"

Sinuha wasn't expecting this question:

"It is true that we mine copper in Sinai and granite in Hamammet. We both use these in our country and sell them to our neighbors. In this matter, the gods have joined forces to help the Pharaoh."

This wasn't the answer that Sepi was expecting, he asked:

"Is it true that you torture them?"

Screwing up his face Sinuha said:

"Yes."

"But why? You make poor people work to the death in sunless underground caves. Isn't this tyranny?"

It was Sinuha's turn to be quiet. Sepi went on:

"Which civilization can exist with tyranny for a long time? Doesn't the highest point of civilization bring decadence with it too?"

Sinuha straightened his inlaid sarong that ended beneath his knees, and looked around carefully. After feeling certain that nobody was listening to them, in a low voice he said:

"Listen Sepi, I'm declaring this fact for the first time to you as a foreigner. Just like my father, I too reject torture."

Sinuha's confession had stimulated the young prince's courage:

"My father told me. Thirty years ago, that is a long time before we were even born, Ramesses had a dream. In his dream, a fire started in our land and even though it spread throughout Egypt, it didn't harm the Israelites at all. That is, as the palaces of Egypt turned into ruins..."

Interrupting his friend, Sinuha said:

"My uncle gathered all the magicians in our country to have his dream interpreted, but none of them wanted to talk. Only one of them said "A child who will be born into the Israelites will ruin Egypt and the Pharaoh." My uncle was terrified upon these words. In those days most Israelites lived in the outskirts on the east side of Memphis. He immediately gave orders: From this moment on, kill all the baby boys that will be born among them."

"Terrifying."

"The men of the Israelites would work in the fields, and the women were servants in our residences. Let's put it this way, they were a miserable lower class."

"What did he do to the baby girls?"

"He left them alone."

"Didn't anyone resist this tyranny?"

"Resist? You can't resist the Pharaoh. He is the absolute ruler of the country, gods' representative on earth. Resisting him is challenging the gods."

"So nobody resisted this tyranny, right?"

"My father came up with an idea: If all the baby boys were to be killed, their population would decrease quickly. Then who would do the work of Egypt? If a solution wasn't found for this our future would be gloomy."

"Your father thought about economy, not the lives of the innocent."

"Don't say that. My father is very compassionate. He couldn't talk in any other way to the Pharaoh."

"History says that a nation can never be annihilated by violence or especially blood. People can only be suppressed with torment and tyranny for a short time. Could your father make the Pharaoh change his mind?"

"A little."

"What do you mean?"

"The babies were killed only every second year. Therefore half of the babies were saved..."

Sinuha stopped talking when he saw the Amun priest Adonis approach them. He took off his sandals made of white leather and decorated with gold paillettes. Stretching out his sweaty feet, he unwillingly smiled at the priest. Greeting them with suspicious eyes, Adonis slowly walked away. The young prince lowered his voice a little more and said:

"All the priests in the academy are spies of the Grand Vizier Haman. He and his men don't like my father at all, and of course me neither. The Grand Vizier is a low flatterer that blindly obeys my uncle. I believe my uncle couldn't find a more suitable helper for himself. Even though he is his brother, my father keeps clear of the Pharaoh. Ramesses has spies everywhere. They hear everything and punish violently. (After Sinuha thought for a while) Haman would detest an Egyptian noble being too familiar with a foreigner, even if it is a prince. He would definitely be skeptical about sedition."

"Our nations are friendly, aren't they? Haven't I been a student of your country for two years?"

"I'm not kidding, don't raise your voice. Egypt's friendship can change at any moment based on the world's situation."

"Sinuha, I really love you."

"And I love you too dear Sepi, and my country too of course. However, unfortunately it is in ruthless hands now."

The son of the Treasurer approached them with a small group of noble Egyptians. Talma, the son of the King of Cyprus, was among them too. To greet them, Talma took the end of his flute away from his mouth. The ear-splitting sound stopped for a moment. But the melody played by Talma had lighted up Sepi's heart:

"Hello fellows, what are you doing? Look at the brightness of that lake, look at the beauty of nature. Stroll around, have fun. Wow. This wonderful view sets my soul on fire, burns my blood, (turning to the group) doesn't it affect you fellows?"

The son of the Treasurer and his friends walked away in joy. The sharp cries of the flute began to echo throughout the plain again.

* * *

The sun had risen high. It was as if a huge blast furnace was boiling in the hills of Faiyum, and flames were pouring from the sky. Everybody had taken shelter under a palm tree. Sinuha loosened his belt one notch more, trying to escape the hot strap on his waist. The sound of a harp could be heard from the woodland a little further on. A quick and lively melody that came to their ears was carrying away the young spirits despite the increasing heat.

Sinuha was excited too. He took his flute out of his bag which was right next to him, and slowly took the end of the cane to his lips. The seriousness of worship had appeared on his face. When he started to move his fingers over the holes, a soft and sad sound covered the plain. The melodies coming from the flute were putting tears in every one's eyes. Sepi's green eyes were wet too, he was crying. The sadness of the song had carried him away. He passed his fingers through his hair and joined them behind his head. Sinuha's sad music would always move him like this.

Two teardrops that rolled off Sinuha's pink cheeks fell on his open chest. He couldn't play it anymore, he took the flute away from his lips and went quiet. His eyes were lost in the blue color of the lake, his looks locked on the water.

Sepi pulled himself together and asked with a soft voice:

"Is it the same girl?"

The young prince didn't answer. He nodded his head unconsciously as if to say "Yes." They didn't talk for a while.

Finally, the young man turned his Nile blue eyes towards his friend with a face in need of mercy. He had dropped his head, he looked like a hopeless patient. All of a sudden he spoke out towards the horizon:

"Look, there it is. A garden full of red flowers in the moonlight. Violets are laughing and talking, looking at the stars. Roses are whispering beautiful scented stories into each other's ears. Naive and clean gazelles are leaping around and listening attentively. In the distance, the water of holy rivers is flowing. I want to lie down in that garden, absorb the silence, and have happy dreams."

After taking a deep breath he continued:

"My beautiful Tiye, I love you more than anything else. I don't want your father's throne, his gold staff or his diamond crown, I want you. Come. I will take you far away on the wings of my music. I know the best of places there."

"Hush Sinuha, please be silent. The pain in your heart hurts me too."

Gathering the skirts of his cloak with his hands, Priest Adonis approached them. He was grimacing from the heat. He looked at them both with suspicion, as if to say "What have you been talking about for hours?" He had either said nothing, or a lot. He silently headed in another direction.

In the late afternoon they were going to leave the lake and return to the campus in Memphis with carriages prepared by the state governor. After all, the purpose of the trip was to show the power of Egypt to foreign students. After Adonis walked away, Sepi moved close to his friend and said:

"Who is this Tiye?"

Sinuha didn't want to talk, but he couldn't resist. He was hoping that his heart would be relieved a little if he talked:

"She is an angel. The shadow of goddess Isis on earth. My dreams are always beautiful with her. When she is with me happiness rains on me. When I look into her eyes all my pain disappears. The hot sun becomes warm, the winds stop, and the flowers in the meadows wink with her."

"Why are you ruining yourself? Your uncle is the most powerful man in Egypt, and isn't your father his brother? Who could stop you rejoining your love?"

"Oh Sepi, my dear friend. You don't know the truth."

"What don't I know?"

"Tiye is the daughter of Grand Vizier Haman."

Sepi was puzzled, he said:

"What bad luck!"

"He hates me. My mercy for slaves drives him crazy. It is as if he is from the same blood as the Pharaoh. He unites with my uncles demons and tyrannizes the innocent."

Sinuha's feelings had changed to hatred of Haman:

"He changed all the ministers. There is no one left in the cabinet other than my father that says that slaves are humans too. If the Israelites are still alive they owe it to my father."

"My father had mentioned Queen Neferure."

The name Neferure lighted up Sinuha's face:

"Yes, the mother of Moses. Queen Mother. Two months ago we celebrated her fortieth birthday. When Moses and I were born, that is twenty three years ago, she was my uncles favorite. My uncle loved her so much that her every wish was considered an order in the palace. He made a magnificent palace in her name, its gardens were full of lotus flowers, and the beauty of its lounges is still talked about in Thebes. I was three years old then. My poor mother came down with a fever and died suddenly. And then ..."

Sinuha's heart filled with grief for his mother. His big blue eyes got watery, his pink face clouded over. He bit his lips and waited for a while, and then he continued:

"Neferure took me into her palace. She is so compassionate, so kind. Did you know Sepi, I grew up with Moses. He is like my full brother."

Sinuha was fondling the red petals of the poppy he had picked unaware, smiling he said:

"We wouldn't listen to our nannies, we would make them all run after us. When we were missing, they would find us by the big pool trying to catch the little red fish. I never separated from him. As you know, we're together in the academy too."

As the subjects changed, Sinuha's face was changing too. All of a sudden in a harsh manner he said:

"That monster called Haman would even be jealous of that angelic woman, and doubt her. As Neferure grew old, he tried to get my uncle interested in others, finally he persuaded the Pharaoh and lured him away from Neferure. My Queen Mother was patient, she endured it all and waited. Did you know Sepi, even though my uncle had numerous children from hundreds of women, he never lost his respect for Queen Mother. Neferure is still the only woman he respects. Even his son Merneptah's mother couldn't wipe her out of the Pharaoh's heart."

"Why was Haman suspicious about the queen?"

"He thought she would influence my uncle. He was guessing that she was trying to reduce the pressure on the Israelites."

"Does Haman's hatred of the Israelites come from the Pharaoh's dream?"

"Not at all, he has a totally different reason. All nobles get their share of profits from the mines. Amun priests, magicians, soldiers, high level bureaucrats. They all build new mansions, beautiful gardens and temples for themselves. The profit grows as much as the Israelites work. Nobody cares about the oppression they face, because as soon as they die, others take their place. That is, Haman and his team only care about the gold they will get."

"So that's how things work in Hamammet."

"After Pharaoh's share is reserved, all of the profit from agriculture and irrigation canals is divided among Haman and his gang. Of course the most powerful gets the biggest share. As you can see, the Israelites are the class that carries the burdens of Egypt. They must work a lot so that Egyptian nobles can enjoy life in their fancy mansions."

"Isn't killing baby boys adverse to this idea?"

"It was stopped about ten years later anyway. Actually, Egypt wants the Israelites to increase at the same rate as they die."

"What do you mean?"

"I mean, the slave population shouldn't increase so much as to threaten Egypt, and it shouldn't decrease so much as to hinder work."

"How subtle. That is the real grounds of its power."

"One of its grounds."

Sepi wanted to change the subject:

"So Tiye is the daughter of this dirty Haman?"

"Yes, my friend, unfortunately."

"Does Tiye know you love her?"

"I think she does."

"What does that mean?"

"We never had a chance to talk, that man prevented it on all occasions."

"Well how did you meet?"

"At the festival for god Min. It is held every year at the beginning of summer. I was in Thebes last June. The people had gathered in the square for the rite of abundance. My uncle climbed on to the hay stacks in front of the temple of Min. After turning to the Min statue which had been brought from the temple and thanking it, he made a speech to the public. Then the holy bull was brought out of the temple in a ceremonial manner and walked past those who had attended the ceremony to be delivered to my uncle."

"What an interesting ceremony."

"My uncle took the white bull by its head, and presented it to god Min."

"Did your uncle talk with the bull?"

Sinuha seemed to have not heard his friends question and said:

"Listen my friend. After presenting the white bull to god Min, my uncle took a wheat ear, bent it in half and held it out to the statue."

Sepi was listening to the story in amazement:

"Did the statue take the wheat ear?"

Sinuha ignored the question and carried on:

"As a part of the ceremony, four white doves were flown in four different directions."

"Why?"

"So that they can announce this holy ceremony to all."

When he looked towards the sky, Sinuha's face changed all of a sudden. He smiled as if he was seeing something. The Prince of Amurru unavoidably looked to the skies too, but he couldn't see anything. Only a hot wind blew in to his face. As if murmuring a sacred prayer, Sinuha quietly asked the prince:

"Do you see her Sepi? There she is, among white tulles. Right in the middle of the other girls. Singing hymns with her beautiful voice. Dancing like an elegant butterfly."

Sinuha's voice had lowered even more, he was murmuring unconsciously:

"Yes, she's getting closer. See Sepi, she's coming towards us. (Pretending to blow things in his hand) I'm blowing the fire red flowers in my hand on to her, petal by petal. Her white clothes are getting covered with red dots all over. I'm reaching out to her, but what is that? All of a sudden she gets on a cloud and flies away, very far away."

"What are you going on about Sinuha, are you losing your mind?"

"Yes, I am losing my mind."

Sunset had set the whole plain on fire, big rocks that covered dots in the distance had become heaps with red lines. All of a sudden deafening sounds from hundreds of horns filled the valley. State messengers were heralding that the Nubia campaign had ended successfully, and that Ramesses was approaching Thebes with thousands of slaves and spoils. The empire's land was growing, and Pharaoh was becoming even more powerful.

Oh Holy Spirit of Apis,
Give Our Country Abundance

a group of twenty five students moved towards the doors of the temple with Priest Adonis, who was guiding them. Astonished they first looked at the embossments at the entrance that illustrated war, and then at the giant Ramesses statues that rose like a mountain before them. Then they entered a deep court which was skirted on three sides by porticos. The length of the court of this Osiris Temple built by Pharaoh was more than one hundred meters.

They went down to the lower level from the staircase with marble steps at the end of the court. It was a dim and cramped place, very little light was trickling through the roof. The embossments and engravings of various gods and goddesses on the wall were dazzling. Reliefs of Egyptian gods had been engraved on the cylindrical pillars in the middle. Embossments had been painted in color, and looked as if they were real.

The academy students silently left the temple and came to the shrine where the Apis bull lived. They passed through a narrow door to a wide court. It was skirted by high walls. All of a sudden they shivered in fear. They had encountered a coal black huge monster of a bull with big horns and its condition could be seen in its muscles. The bull was being walked under supervision of a young priest in great respect.

Sinuha whispered in to Sepi's ear:

"This is the Apis bull you were wondering about."

"But this is an ordinary bull that could be seen in any meadow."

Trying not to lose his temper Sinuha said:

"No Sepi, no. It is a god. It is a god carrying the spirit of Osiris in its body. It gives abundance to Egypt by flowing the sweet water of the Nile continuously."

Looking like he was surprised, Sepi said:

"Is it so."

"See, there are silver marks on its back. (After pausing for a moment) Do you see the white triangle sign on its head?"

"These things you mentioned can be found on many bulls."

"The tail hair must be double. And there should also be a pattern like a cockroach on its tongue."

Sinuha raised his voice upon his friend's negligence:

"The only bull on earth created with these features."

"What do you do when it dies?"

"The Amun priests in Memphis travel to all the villages in the country without losing time, they use all means available for this holy mission, to find the new holy bull."

"I thought there was only one of them in the whole world."

"When it dies the gods create another one."

"You have interesting beliefs."

Without making obvious that he was getting tired Sinuha said:

"Apis bulls are taken care of with great attention. Expert priests walk them in the court at certain times throughout the day. Oracles make something out of its every move."

With a devilish smile Sepi said:

"Do you count the tail hairs of a bull to regard it a god?"

- ....

The bull with white spots on its back that was breathing flames through its nostrils was swinging its horns around in a dangerous way, putting its caretaker on the spot.

"Has the holy bull ever gored a priest?"

Tired of the questions, the young prince mumbled:

"I don't know."

They left the court upon the priest's warning. A little further ahead, a narrow doorway leading underground could be seen. With torches made of papyrus stalks in their hands, straight away they noticed the Serapeum priests at the door. Following them they went down to the gallery where the Apis mummies were. In the dimly lit gallery there were many tombs made of granite lined up.

Sepi moved close to Sinuha and asked:

"Do you bury the bulls that die here?"

"Yes.

- ....

The death of Apis is a great disaster for Egypt. That day mourning is declared in the country, the whole nation cries together, ceremonies start in temples. The most magnificent funeral ceremony is held in this temple with the attendance of the Pharaoh too. The honorable Apis is mummified carefully, and put in a stone tomb in this temple."

Sepi was having a hard time trying not to burst out laughing. However, Sinuha hadn't noticed his mimics in the dimly lit gallery, and was continuing to guide him:

"General mourning goes on for days until the new Apis is found, when the new one shows up it takes over the mission, that is, it is accepted that the old totem hasn't died, and that it is alive."

"You have weird customs my friend."

"When Apis is brought to the temple the festival begins. All over the country festivals are held, ceremonies are conducted, and gifts are given to the public. Tens of thousands of Egyptians rush to this temple, they almost attack it to see the new bull, and be blessed by it. Hundreds of people get crushed to death in the crowd."

The pontiff's deep voice echoed off the thick walls of the temple:

"O Holy Apis' glorious spirits! Give our Pharaoh strength, and our country abundance!"

The Egyptian students bowed in great respect in front of the tombs. The prince of Amurru whispered in to Sinuha's ear:

"Do you believe that these dead bulls can help you?"

"Yes Sepi, they carry the spirit of Osiris."

Save Me God of Joseph

O holy Nile, I salute you,
You come to give Egypt life.
As you spread over the land of Ra,
Songs of joy are sung everywhere.

While Sinuha was singing this most popular folk song about the Nile on his chestnut horse, he was trying to shake off the slackness of the last days at school too. Days of returning to Thebes, and rejoining his Tiye getting closer increased the uncontrollable excitement in his heart, he was often day dreaming, walking around unaware of what he was doing.

The weight of the hot and overwhelming air could be felt, sweat was dripping off their faces. Even though shadows had grown long, the heat wasn't decreasing, they were both preparing to take a break at the first shade they came across.

* * *

It was near evening. They had left the academy with the first lights of dawn, drawing a wide arc they had drifted away from the Nile, and rode their horses through the desert eastbound all day long. They were intending to see the Red Sea which they had longed for years to see up close. The Red Sea was the natural border of the country in the east. Sinai could be entered by going around the harbor from the north. There, in the middle of the desert, there were rich copper reserves where prisoners and slaves worked. They had heard that Egypt's ships on the coast carried minerals nonstop from one shore to the other.

According to their calculations they didn't have much more to go. They were thinking they would be leaving the dry land of the desert soon. However, they weren't expecting it to be that hot. The sun was pouring flames on them from the sky. They had to find a place to cool down. The high temperature had made the animals exhausted and devastated too.

The palm trees that vaguely appeared a little later on the horizon were the sign of water and shade. Finally, the oasis had come in sight.

Sinuha joyfully shouted:

"Hey, there it is. The end of the Knife District."

Moses rose majestically on his piebald horse, shading his eyes with his left hand he looked towards the horizon:

"Look southeast of the palm trees. Can you see the caravan?"

"Yes, something's going on there."

"We'll pass close soon."

Moses was a tall, olive skinned, handsome young man with strong black hair. He was strong and brave, however he was rather harsh.

* * *

Cloud banks flying scattered in the sky were attracting attention. With the zeal of getting close to the oasis they whipped their horses harshly. They were proceeding towards the caravan. Despite all the insistence of those who were liable, they didn't want anyone with them, they had left as if escaping from Memphis. After all, it was their last day at the academy, they had completed their education. First they were going to go straight to El Teb, to attend the festival for the Pharaoh's Nubia success, and then they were going to be appointed to important missions in either El Teb or Pi Ramesses by Pharaoh Ramesses.

They were safe in Egypt. They thought they would reach the garrison on the coast before night fell. They were going to be guests there for a few days, embrace the harsh waves of the Red Sea and return. Moses had wanted to do this trip, the Red Sea was his irrevocable passion. For some reason he had dreamed of the land on the other side of the Red Sea since his childhood, he had a longing for there for an unknown reason.

They had come about four to five hundred meters close to the caravan slowly on its way to Memphis, even though it was going in the opposite direction, they had followed it. The magnitude of the caravan was glamorous. Slightly lifting the striped cover over his eyes Sinuha said:

"Magnificent wealth."

Moses had his eyes on the red flags of the caravan:

"It belongs to Korah" he murmured.

"The man knows how to make a profit."

"It's due to his partnership with Haman."

"How can he be so rich even though he is an Israelite?"

"Because he is low and treacherous."

"The front of the caravan has reached Memphis but we still haven't reached the end of it."

"On every return he passes his caravan through the main streets of Memphis or Thebes in magnificence, shows his strength to all. I think he has a political aim."

"Could he be playing for Haman's position?"

"Why not?"

"He is smart enough to understand that."

"But you forget what Haman has less than Korah."

"Gold."

"I'm glad you understood."

"But Korah is an Israelite."

"Is there a door that a fortune wouldn't open? He now lives like a Copt, thinks like a Copt, and acts like a Copt. His being an Israelite has no importance at all."

"He wears shiny clothes, uses expensive jewelry, and rubs on nice scents. His being seen frequently at mansion parties is an extension of this thought."

"He's preparing the terms to gather everyone around him."

"Isn't this dangerous for his own future?"

"Those who have an ambition, accept the dangers."

There was no sign of them being princes other than their medals around their necks, but they couldn't be seen because they were under their vests. They had come to the edge of Knife District as ordinary people. They liked it that way, they felt more comfortable. When they reached the oasis, they washed their whole body starting from their faces with the water they drew from the deep well in the shade of the palm trees. They ate the cheesy pastry they had in the bags tied to their saddles.

The two friends had been studying management at the academy for the past four years together. Moses was popular in sportive activities. He was an irresistible young man with his strong muscles, brute force and outstanding courage. Forget humans, not even a cow could stand the strength of his fist. The Prince of Amurru was their mutual friend, they thought similarly on many matters. They would revolt against tyranny and injustice together, and wanted every person to be treated equally and fair, whatever their social status was. The contradictions and deviance in Egypt's religion caught their attention. They promised each other that they would strive to correct the situation throughout their life, and took an oath of allegiance.

Even though Moses was the Pharaoh's son, which meant being a prince, for some reason Ramesses didn't like him. It was the same for Moses too. He couldn't love his father either, actually it could be said that he hated him. The puzzling distance between father and son was at a level that everybody around them could notice. Moses was ashamed of being the son of such a tyrant father. That was the principle emotion that alienated him from his father. He had been studying away from home, in Memphis, since he was a small child. When he went south in the holidays to see his mother, his father would be in the summer time palace in Pi Ramesses; when he arrived there the Pharaoh would have been gone to Thebes. In short, they hardly saw each other for a day or two in a year, and that wouldn't be longer than a few hours.

In the years when Thebes was the capital, ships flying the Amun flag would leave the port escorted by a priest with ceremonies every year, and would visit all the colonies along the Nile. Gilded ships would stop if the oracles chose to, a priest or his high ranking magician would go ashore, and select one or a few of the children born that year as candidates for The School of Priests. These children would leave their families for the rest of their lives with the ship departing from the village. Because it was considered that this selection would honor the village people, a festival would be organized and the child's family would be accounted honorable. When the candidates were brought to Thebes they would be raised to be servants in temples, and some of them in palaces of the Pharaoh or other nobles. Even though he spent his childhood in a palace, Moses would say that he felt like a stranger; he would compare himself to these poor village children that got taken away from their houses. Moses' voice had involuntarily risen:

"I'm just like them."

"Who?"

"The poor children that the magicians collect."

"Why?"

"Who else loves me but my mother?"

Imhotep's son was his only shoulder to cry on:

"Come on, we've lost enough time here. We should be at the garrison before dark."

Moses separated a papyrus from the roll he took out of his bag. It was a map. The arms of the Nile, oases, swamps and the garrison on the Red Sea Coast had all been marked on it with colorful pencils. Sinuha opened the map, holding his hands like a tent, he put his fingertips on the surface. Thus he was preventing the map from scrolling. And Moses put his index finger on the oasis. That was where they were. Then he moved his hand towards the east to the garrison. There were no obstacles on their way other than the small swamp which appeared considerably south.

"We should hurry" they both said at the same time.

They were both riding their horses and shouting at one another to be heard.

Sinuha cried out at the top of his lungs:

"I've missed Queen Mother a lot."

"Me too."

"I miss Thebes only because of her."

"Me too."

"We're like twins, aren't we Moses?"

"Yes."

"You take me as your full brother, don't you?"

"Yes."

"I love you Moses."

"And I love you Sinuha."

"I invited Sepi to the festival."

"Why?"

"He should get to know Egypt better."

They were communicating by shouting because the noise of the horses' hooves was smothering their voice. As they got closer to the coast it cooled down a bit, and a breeze had begun. The clouds that appeared in the sky and flew around like black spots were increasing, and running too as if they were trying to catch up with them. Sinuha's voice was heard:

"Sepi questioned Apis on our last trip, and asked what we were expecting from a black bull."

"..."

"Do you hear me Moses? What do you say? Sometimes I think like him too. Why do you think we worship a bull?"

* * *

It was rather dark, the pitch black had taken over the plain, not a single light could be seen. The last palm trees of the oasis were far behind. All of a sudden a large raindrop fell on Sinuha's nose. Then another. The air had cooled down dramatically. They hadn't taken their red cloaks so that they wouldn't be identified as academy students. They had taken blue cloaks just like the public and whipped their horses. The harsh wind that had started to blow in the dark plain was getting even more intense, it was giving the first signs of a severe storm.

In the silence of the night spooky cracking noises could be heard from the branches that broke and fell off trees. Little pieces of branches and leaves that were flying around were hitting their faces. The large raindrops first wet their heads, and then their whole bodies, in a few minutes they were soaked. After a short silence, the plain shook with such a horrible sound that the horses neighed in fear and reared up despite their riders efforts. All of a sudden the cloud above them burst. Such a flood started that in a short time they found themselves in the middle of a big sea. The rain was torrential, as if a secret hand had brought the Nile on top of them. They couldn't make way anymore, they were hopelessly trying to swim with their horses in the middle of the wild flood. The storm and rain was devastating everywhere, the wide plain was being pounded by water, and the skies were pouring down on earth. Among the scary roaring Sinuha's cry was heard:

"Moses, we're lost."

The young prince didn't get an answer. Hours went by, each minute as long as a century. The storm was lightening but the rain kept on pouring down to drown the plain. The horses' hooves were sometimes touching hard ground and sometimes struggling with the water. Despite the weather cooling down the animals were sweaty, their tired breaths could be heard from the other end of the plain. In fear, Sinuha cried out again:

"Moses, where are you?"

"I'm over here."

The voice of Moses had relieved him:

"What shall we do?"

In a sarcastic manner, Moses said:

"Pray to Apis."

"You're crazy."

Among the sound of the rain the laughter of Moses was heard.

* * *

Hours had gone by but they hadn't found the garrison yet. They couldn't see a step ahead anyway. They were totally being led by their horses. Sinuha's voice was heard again:

"Maybe we went past the garrison in the dark. Now we're going to spend the long night under this rain that is getting heavier."

Sinuha's wet clothes had stuck to his body tightly. His whole body was shaking, he was freezing. He tried calling out to Moses:

"Hey!"

Just at that moment he realized that his horse was sinking. The ground was mushy, soft sounds were coming from the mud. The animal was having difficulty getting its hooves out of the mud. He stiffly tightened the reins and whipped his horse. He had started a hopeless struggle in the dark under the terrible heavy rain. He was hitting the animal's rear with the whip he had hanging off his saddle, thinking it was now or never. He was repetitively and ruthlessly whipping the poor animal.

He had never considered dying this way. The thought of soon being sucked in by the soft mud beneath his feet, being pulled under the surface froze his blood. He remembered that he had to pray to get out of this situation. However he was facing a weird feeling that he didn't confess to Moses, Sepi, or anyone else. He didn't want to pray to Apis bull, sun god Amun, nor his twin children Thoth or goddess Maat. He didn't trust them. He visualized the ugly face of the devious priest that had followed him on the shore of Faiyum. He screamed out "I'm not afraid of you." He wasn't afraid of Anubis, the jackal headed god of death either. He wasn't going to ask for their help. He was whipping his horse, and at the same time thinking who he was going to ask for help.

Tiye's garden decorated with lotus flowers came to his mind. The girl that he loved was calling from among colorful flowers, telling him not to be afraid. He almost heard the compassionate princess whisper in to his ear "come on, you're going to pull through." He tried to look around through the mixture of rain and sweat on his face, but he couldn't see anybody. However he now had hope that he would get out of this marsh.

Tears added to the wetness on his face. He was repeating Tiye's name. The chestnut mare was pounding the ground with all its strength, fighting the mud, breathing deeply. Was he going to make his way out of this marsh?

And now Neferure came to his mind. He murmured "Oh my dear Queen Mother." He had remembered her mentioning a Prophet named Joseph years ago. Should he, as she secretly did, take refuge in the God of the Israelites? He went deep in to his memory. This is what he remembered:

Five hundred years ago, the north of Egypt, the Delta, was invaded by a foreign nation. They came from Syria and invaded Memphis, they had taken advantage of domestic disturbance and taken control of the whole of Egypt. They were called The Hyksos, Shepherd Kings. This nation was the forefathers of the Amurru's.

One of their kings had a smart vizier by the name of Joseph, who wasn't of their nation. This vizier that was responsible for the treasury saved the country from famine, and reconstructed Egypt from one end to the other. He worshiped a single God that he believed created everything, and called him "Allah." He brought the tribe led by his father Jacob to Egypt. They called their leader Israel too. From those days till now the Israelites only believe in Him, and in hardship only ask for His help, and only rely on Him.

* * *

Queen Mother would say that Joseph was a Prophet, that is, the one and only God had sent him to people as a Messenger.

Sinuha was trying to remember what the Queen had said.

When the vizier saved the country from famine, the king gave him a crown decorated with pearls and rubies, and a gold throne. Joseph looked at the crown and throne and said "Let's strengthen our country with the jewels on these." As he didn't accept the crown given by the king, he refused to sit on the throne too.

Couldn't the God of that great person who saved Egypt from that disaster save me from this marsh I am stuck in? His horse's hooves were hopelessly struggling in the sea of mud and sinking more in the marsh every minute. He started to shout at the top of his lungs:

"Save me God of Joseph."

However it happened, suddenly his horses hooves stepped on a hard piece of soil. The animal got itself out of the marsh with one last effort; he was saved. Sinuha was confused. He was holding on tight to his horse, as if they were one. He couldn't figure out how he escaped so easily. What had happened, how had it happened? How had he escaped this hopeless situation? Had the God of Joseph really helped him, or was it a coincidence? He thought for a few seconds. No, it couldn't be a coincidence. This sudden escape from death, just when he was being slowly pulled towards the bottom of the mud, could not be a coincidence.

"Queen Mother, your path is the right one" he cried out.

The man who was said to be a Prophet had helped him, the God of Joseph had saved him. He totally believed this. Now he felt grateful to that God he never knew, he felt in his heart that he was close to Him.

All of a sudden he remembered Moses. His heart was beating as if it was going to jump out of his skin. Was he still alive? It was still pitch black, and the rain was continuing to pour down. He tried to push his long hair that had stuck to his face to the back of his head. Worried, he cried out a few times:

"Moses! Moses!"

He didn't get an answer to his call. His heart was about to stop. He shouted again with a loud voice:

"Moses! Moses!"

This time he seemed to hear a faint answer from the distance.

"Sinuha!"

He was relieved. He rode his horse wildly in the direction of the voice. A little later he heard the neighing of the piebald horse next to him. He asked excitedly:

"How did you survive?"

Sinuha couldn't notice the astonishment of Moses in the pitch dark.

"Survive what?"

"The marsh."

"What marsh? We only lost each other in the storm and rain."

Sinuha went quiet, he hadn't understood anything. They were randomly riding their horses in a direction they didn't know. Among the sound of the rain the voice of Moses was heard:

"Do you see the light?"

Sinuha answered with a tired voice:

"Yes."

"Come on then, let's go there."

The horses headed towards the light upon their masters orders.

Tears Running from His Eyes Were Running towards His Neck

*B*arking dogs could be heard. They assumed they had come to a small farm. A few men with torches in their hands ran towards them trying to understand what was happening. However the heavy rain was putting out their torches one by one. A tall man in his forties welcomed them. The man who said his name was Abel gave the tired horses to the men with him, and then took them through a wide court skirted by high walls. They entered a long and narrow room. In the dim light of torches made of papyrus fiber, it was obvious that it was a modest place. Old felt covers that were obviously home-made covered the floor, there were low sofas along the walls and an old armchair had been placed in the corner.

Even though it was summer, the storm outside was continuing. A large and strong man had brought them things to wear so they could change their wet clothes. They had just sat on the sofas with their new clothes when Abel entered the room with a big tray full of food. Bread with goose fat spread on, beef jerky, bean puree, fried eggs, cheese and honey was going to satisfy their hunger. The man wasn't talking at all, he only served.

While Moses and Sinuha were heartily eating their fill, they were also looking around the room in curiosity, trying to understand where they were. It must have been a village house. They decided to hide their identity because nobody was happy about the Pharaoh's tyranny, they could be harmed. They were Syrian students studying in Memphis. They had lost their way in the storm on their way home. Sinuha's name was Zet, and Moses' name was Uni. Even though they scanned the walls of the room carefully, they couldn't see any god statues that could be found in Egyptian houses.

Sinuha quietly said:

"That's weird, there aren't any god statues."

Moses interpreted the situation in a different way:

"They aren't Copts, they must be Israelites."

Abel who entered the room again kindly asked:

"Who are you, what are you doing here in this weather?"

Sinuha calmly said:

"My name is Zet, and this is Uni. We are Syrian, we're studying in Memphis. We had come to see the Red Sea. I think we got lost."

"Were you going to the garrison?"

"Correct."

"You've gone too far south. You look tired. Rest a few days and recover. I will take you there."

They both considered that they had come to the region without permission, and that they couldn't stay in a stranger's house long.

Meanwhile, an old hunchbacked man with white hair entered the room. He made his way slowly, leaning on his thick staff, and settled in the old armchair in the corner of the room. The torch right next to him lighted half of his face with its flickering light. All the pain he had suffered throughout his life could be read in the deep lines on his face. The young men looked like they were busy eating, but they were looking at the old man from the corner of their eyes. All of a sudden Moses turned to Abel and said:

"You must be Israelites."

It couldn't be seen that Abel had turned pale because of the flickering light in the room that mixed colors. He slightly smiled. He was trying to quietly catch his father's looks. When there was no change in the old man's attitude, Abel was relieved. Trying not to let his voice shake he said:

"What makes you say that?"

"There aren't any god statues in your room."

Sinuha said:

"There are god statues in every house in Thebes."

Abel calmly said:

"Oh, really?"

They had finished their meal. When the young man left the room to take the tray, the old man talked with a voice that could hardly be heard:

"You two look like careful and smart young men."

His voice was shaking, and he was stopping between sentences:

"I want to ask you something. What are statues good for?"

Even though he didn't believe it himself, Sinuha repeated what he had learned from oracles:

"They are symbols of god. Without them, who would see us, who would hear us, who would help us? We need them to pray."

When Sinuha understood that the old man was listening to him quietly, he continued to tell what he knew:

"Creatures live after death too, but there is a requirement for this. The body must be mummified and preserved as it is. Moreover, mummification isn't sufficient for eternity. Statues of the deceased must be made out of durable materials like bone, wood, stone or gold, and these statues that show the shape of the deceased in their health should be buried with them."

Trying not to catch Moses' eyes:

"When spirits go to the other world, they go to Anubis, the god of death, and enter their statues under his stern looks. Anubis is the son of Amun, the Sun god. If this awesome god cannot be conciliated, there is no way you can enter Aaru, the fields of heaven, you will go straight to hell."

The old man took over:

"You look like rich people. As you know, the rich never put statues in their graves. Instead, they bury their servants or slaves they buy from the slave market. They use live material, in the other world they work their spirits in Aaru fields. In the fields of heaven, slaves work, Pharaohs rest under fig trees. Rough earthenware statues are only put in the graves of the poor, aren't they?"

The sound like whip lashes on the roof had stopped. That meant that the rain had stopped. As the old man talked he had opened up, and got his breath back:

"Listen young man, your friend guessed right, we are of the Israelites. Our forefather Israel gathered his children in his last hours, and asked who they would worship from then on. They answered 'We will obey and worship the God of you and our forefathers, Abraham and Ishmael, and not accept any other.' They were Prophets, Messengers of God, the creator of the universe. However, great happiness can only be reached after great pain in this world. For example, Prophet Joseph became the saint of Egypt after many disasters."

When Sinuha heard the name "Joseph" he shivered. He couldn't wait to get to know the person who had just saved him from the marsh, he had a great desire for it. However, he had to hide this emotion. How much could they trust a stranger? If the Pharaoh heard about this conversation, it would be the end of him. Even his father could be punished for this. But he really wanted to learn the truth, and Moses was thinking alike.

The old man went on:

"Joseph was taken in to the palace of Egypt after spending a long time in a dark well, and then his long pris-on life started, he lived for years away from his family."

The old man sighed deeply:

"Joseph is the son of Prophet Jacob, who is also known as Israel. He had been brought to the position of treasury secretary five hundred years ago due to his services to Egypt, and declared a saint. He requested permission from the king to bring his tribe. When his request was accepted his longing which went on for years came to an end, he was happy. He was ruling the whole of Egypt, getting everything he wanted. We, the Israelites, are the descendants of these great people. We believe in his God, Who is the one and only, and created the universe, and we accept Joseph to be His Messenger, a Prophet."

He looked like he was deep in thought, and he was murmuring words that couldn't be understood every now and then. Meanwhile, Abel, who had entered the room went straight to his father and whispered something in his ear. By his attitude it was obviously an important matter. However the old man didn't seem to hear him. Wrapping himself in his cloak he started to talk again:

"Prophet Abraham asked his tribe what they worshiped. They said that they believed in statues and that they were proud of it. Upon this, Abraham said that statues were unconscious and irresolute pieces of stone or wood, and that they weren't even aware that they were worshiping them. You are smart, how can you expect help from these lifeless things? They cannot give you provisions, and they can't take you to heaven. They have no power at all."

The two young men had clearly understood the absurdity of worshiping black bulls and statues with jackal heads. As he was unconsciously moving his hand around on his bare chest Sinuha jumped all of a sudden. Flames had licked his face. The royal medallion wasn't around his neck. He murmured "I must have dropped it while struggling in the marsh."

The old man hadn't noticed Sinuha's fear. With difficulty he stood up, and trying to straighten his bending back with the help of his right hand he said:

"Which one of you is Sinuha?"

They remembered saying that their names were Zet and Uni. Or was this old man a magician? They didn't answer for a while. Only the splashes of the non-stopping rain could be heard in the room.

Sinuha murmured "Just like the Pharaoh's magicians." His heart was full of fear. Because he thought there was no importance in keeping his name a secret anymore he said:

"Me."

Old Ezekiel held out the gold medallion in his hand to him and said:

"This must be yours."

He was both surprised and happy. He wasn't a magician, he knew his name from the embossment on the medallion. He reached out and took the medallion, its chain had broken off. His lie was exposed, he felt his face turn pink. Fortunately the room wasn't well lit.

"Young man, do you know the meaning of your name?"

Sinuha was glad that the subject had changed, he started to talk:

"Sir, when the Great Amenhotep who built the Memphis Dam and captured the Nile in its riverbed died, his son was on an expedition. When he heard about his father's death he cancelled the expedition and returned to Memphis immediately. However, some people in the palace were preparing for a rebellion. A friend of the deceased Pharaoh, Sinuha, fled the country assuming that he was doubted too, he went to Asian deserts and took refuge in a Bedouin tribe. A while later he married the beautiful daughter of the chief."

Sinuha had remembered Tiye and gulped. He stopped, and took a deep breath, he had managed to conceal his pain:

"The chief of the tribe gave him a lot of land, and made him his assistant. Sinuha made a big fortune in a short time, he became very rich, but he wasn't happy. He couldn't get over his homesickness. He got to a stage that he was thinking about his country nonstop. He was praying to gods every day, crying out 'O Amun, I want to die in my own homeland.' Finally his desire crossed the desert and reached the ear of Pharaoh Sesostris. The Pharaoh gave orders for him to be taken back in to the palace; after all, he knew that he was innocent. Sinuha spent the rest of his life as the king's best friend. Such that, when he died the Pharaoh even had a huge stone tomb made in his name. My father named me Sinuha in commemoration of this patriotic and noble person who would cry of homesickness."

"You must be the son of Imhotep."

Sinuha was shocked once again. How could this lonely man on the shore of the Red Sea know his father?

Ezekiel turned to Moses:

"Young man, you must be from the palace too."[1]

Bitter Screams

Moses didn't worship statues either. He believed in the God of Joseph, that is Allah. He felt a causeless and deep warmth for the old man in his heart. He hadn't even shared his thoughts that only Queen Mother knew with Sinuha yet, he would criticize Egyptian gods when he was with him, but he wouldn't take it too far. Now he was unable to contain himself, for some reason, he want-

---

[1]   Erman A., *L'egiypte des Pharaons*, Paris, 1939, p. 142.

ed to open up all the secrets of his heart to this old man that they had just met.

"My name is Moses, I am the son of the Pharaoh."

Whenever he said that he was the son of the Pharaoh, his clean spirit would be tormented, but how else could he introduce himself? He felt like he had a share in all of his sins, because he came from the blood of such a tyrant man. He had confessed his sin once again. He lowered his head and went quiet.

It was the old man's turn to be surprised. He wanted to say something, but he couldn't talk. His mouth was locked, he had turned pale. Abel was shocked too. He had never seen his father like this before. What was going on? Who was Moses, the son of the Pharaoh? Why had his name excited his father so much? All of a sudden he said:

"Father, father."

Ezekiel raised his hands as if to say "Don't worry." The young men were watching the old man with empty eyes.

Nothing but the tapping sound of large raindrops falling off leaves on to the roof could be heard in the room. The barking of dogs had stopped a long time ago. After a long pause, the old man held the sides of the armchair with his wrinkled hands and slowly wriggled. With a voice that those in the room could hardly hear he said:

"Here they know me as Absalom, but my name is Ezekiel. It was years ago. I had a furniture shop in Thebes. One day Pharaoh Seti, the father of Ramesses, called me to the palace and requested me to make a perfect throne. He had an artist's spirit, he liked my work so much that he took me in to the palace. I was making lounge suites and inlaid trunks. I would sculpt the legs of the sofas as antelope legs, and sometimes as lion legs. My wife was a carving master, she would shape ivory with great care, and she worked mainly in the queen's quarters. When Pharaoh Seti died, Ramesses took his place. At first he treated me kindly, but later he changed."

After a deep breath, the old man continued:

"All Pharaohs are candidates to be a god, they believe they will be real gods after they die. However, Ramesses went further than his forefathers. He announced himself a god when he was yet a young man at the age of twenty two. He said that he was immortal, and that he repre-sented the gods. One day he said 'I am your lord', and he sent to prison and tortured those who didn't accept him as their lord. Even though the priests objected at first, they later took their place by his side. They had to do this for their own benefit. They were beginning their magic and spells by saying 'In the name of our Lord Pharaoh.' Flattery was well rewarded. Pharaoh used religion and money as a political instrument to increase his power, he gave generously to those who absolutely obeyed him. He even announced that priesthood and wizardry would descend from father to son."

Sinuha couldn't overcome his curiosity:

"Didn't the army interfere at all?"

"Ramesses had formed a new army of guards in Thebes in the name of god Ptah, he went everywhere with them. One reason for the Pharaoh being influential was the Nile. Ramesses had placed his loyal men with appropriate intervals along the river in many strategic spots, and prevented probable rebellions. He was terrorizing the whole country with the help of his Grand Vizier Haman, he killed hundreds of Egyptians that didn't accept him as their lord by torture. He placed giant statues of himself in cities. He wanted the people to show the same respect they showed to him, to his statues too. Ceremonies were held and animals were sacrificed in front of these statues. During one of these ceremonies he said to the people 'O my people! Aren't Egypt and these rivers that run through it mine?'

The people were being impressed by this magnificence, he had managed to make people believe that he was god."

The young men from Memphis were listening to Ezekiel's words in great amazement. Even though it was late, and they were tired, they were still fresh. Moses was listening to the things told about his father in great sorrow.

The old man continued with his speech:

"A long time ago the Israelites had equal opportunities with Egyptians. In time, rulers felt discomfort about this and provoked the locals against us, we were exposed to a lot of pressure from the Copts. For example, when

Pharaoh Ramesses came to throne at the age of sixteen, he claimed that the Nile flowed with his permission and closed the canals that went to the land of the Israelites. Therefore our crops were desiccated, our fields became barren. Then we became slaves on our own land. Our profits were going to the treasury of the Pharaoh, those who raised their voice were put in prison, tortured, and most of them were brutally killed. Grand Vizier Haman had even surpassed the Pharaoh in atrocity. Tyrants were ruling, only Imhotep was left in the cabinet from the previous one."

The old man glanced at Sinuha. The young blond man cursed to have loved such a man's daughter, however his heart didn't listen to him. He murmured "When I look in to her eyes all my pain disappears, when I hug her all the happiness in the sky rains on me." He would like to annihilate Haman's disgusting body at once, to strangle him with his own hands; however, his uncle wasn't much different than him. He thought that even though he was his father, Moses probably hated him too. Then he looked over the face of the old man who was fearlessly talking under the dim light. How heedless he was. He said to himself "He must have lost his mind, who does he count on." All of a sudden; he said "The God of Joseph of course," and smiled. "Since their God that I hesitated to believe in even saved me from the marsh, why couldn't he help the old man," he said.

The flames of the torches on the wall were gradually fading, but the old man was determined to continue:

"Young men were taken from their houses, divided into groups and given to the order of district governors. They were sometimes used for breaking granite in Hammamat, and sometimes in copper mines. The Pharaoh was getting worse every day, he was oppressing and torturing our nation in the worst way. Only because the Israelites believed in a single God and accepted Abraham as a Prophet. We didn't accept the divinity of Amun, jackal headed Anubis, Holy Bull, the Pharaoh or goddess Sekhmet with a lioness' body."

The old man's past had been brought up. His memories were lining up one after another. He couldn't give up any of his memories, he was striving to pass on all that he knew without skipping anything.

"One day the Pharaoh gave an order. Statues of him and the other gods were to be kept in every house. Houses that didn't have statues were being demolished, those who said they didn't worship them would be punished violently. Saying 'Allah' was a crime. Those who said they believed in the God of Prophet Abraham or Joseph weren't left alive. The Pharaoh didn't accept any thought other than being worshiped. Flatterers who said that Ramesses created them were brought to high positions. A man hunt had started, oppression and violence was spreading. Resisters' eyes were gouged out, ears and tongues were cut off, hands and feet were nailed. Hundreds of our cognates were thrown into fires. My wife and I were watching it all in fear. But we weren't going to apostatize from God's religion."

Ezekiel stopped, he was tired; but he started again:

"One day disaster knocked on our door too. We were arrested and thrown into the prison of the palace upon a scoundrel's notification. My wife and I were put in separate cells. There were hundreds of prisoners waiting for death like me, in the terrible prison near the palace of Thebes. One day, in the middle of the night, the metal door of the cell opened with a creepy sound. We had all jumped up in fear. Everybody was trying to guess whose turn it was. All of a sudden the deep voice of the head guard was heard.

'Ezekiel, come here.' So it was my turn to die, I was shaking. I stumbled up the dark stairs. I was taken to Queen Neferure, the devoted woman who brought you up. She was the Pharaoh's favorite then, her every wish was taken as an order. After sending off the guards, she took me into a small room and quietly said:

'Ezekiel, I'm going to save you.'

I was surprised. How could she dare to do such a thing, why was she putting herself on the line for me? She was a beautiful girl, only seventeen years old. She had blonde hair and green eyes. Ramesses almost worshiped her, he loved her madly. What would happen if the Pharaoh found out? I couldn't bear the consequences. I was over the age of fifty, I had lived a long time.

I begged 'Let me be a martyr, I shall die for God, do not risk yourself for me', however she didn't listen to me. She didn't know the Pharaoh well enough, she trusted his love. When I realized resisting was useless, I accepted it. I was thinking about my wife, she had just turned thirty five. I knelt down and cried.

'My dear queen' I said. 'What about my dear Rispa?'

To my surprise, the Pharaoh was in Hammamat that day on inspection. With great courage, she said:

'Do not worry, I will send her after you.'

'Please consider yourself.' I said, and started to beg again. She frowned and said:

'I order you as your queen.' She was so full of kindness, ordering didn't suit her at all.

'Come on Ezekiel, you don't have much time. You have to be on the east of the Nile before the Pharaoh gets back. Two of my men will take you to a rowboat on the shore. You will cross the river yourself, a strong horse is waiting there for you. Go to the Valley of Kings, and hide there. Egyptians can never go there.'

Smiling and quietly:

'Because the spirits of their gods will strike them.' she said.

I had understood that my dear queen didn't believe in Egyptian gods.

'After the Valley of Kings, go south towards Punt, and wait at the first oasis you come across. I shall send Rispa in a few days.'

'What if the Pharaoh returns?'

'No, he will go to the Red Sea. He won't be back before a week.'

I left immediately, and reached Kombala Oasis on the way to Punt the following evening. All I needed was in the bag tied to the horse's saddle. Most importantly, shiny Egyptian gold with embossments of the Pharaoh on them. I was supposed to be an Egyptian tradesman waiting for his caravan to come from the south of Punt.

Even though I spent more than a week there, there was no news from Rispa. My heart was full of fear. I was worried about my wife, my children and the Queen. My Abel was twelve years old then. He was staying with my friend Imran, in a village three miles south of Thebes."

The old man looked at Abel affectionately:

"I had sent him to the village because he was getting tired of the restrictions in the palace, the others were with my wife. My eldest daughter was six, my son was nine, and my tiny daughter Abigail was three years old. They had been imprisoned with Rispa too. If you had only seen Abigail. She was a very cute girl, her blonde hair would fall on her small and round shoulders, and she had tiny plump arms. She would sleep with a faint smile on her pink face. When she opened her Nile blue eyes she would joyfully jump into her mother's arms, and get many kisses from her. I can't tell you how happy I was at her birth when I heard that she was a girl."

Ezekiel went quiet for a long while. The torches on the wall kept on burning, giving off sooty smoke.

"Because the year she was born was the year of killing baby boys, if she wasn't a girl she was going to be killed too. I waited for Rispa the second week too, but she didn't come. I hadn't received any news from Egypt either. I would sometimes sit and cry, and sometimes be lost in thought. Not knowing what to do I wandered around. I couldn't stand it anymore. I decided to return to Thebes at the risk of being thrown in to fire, and set off immediately. When I was close to the Valley of Kings I waited for the night to fall. When it got dark, I took refuge in a graveyard. The fate of my beloved ones was gnawing at me. What had happened to Rispa, why hadn't my children come, had they lost their way? I didn't even want to think about the possibility of the Pharaoh finding out about the situation. When my eyes shut from fatigue, I saw my tiny girl Abigail in my dream. 'Daddy', she said and hugged me, 'Save us', she was yelling madly. I woke in horror. I was murmuring 'O God help me, O glorious Abraham, help me!' These must have been nightmares made by my delusions. I was struggling not to sleep, but I couldn't keep my eyes open. Then I saw Rispa. She was in a beautiful garden on the shore of the Nile, smiling among flowers. Prophet Abraham was with her too. When I reached out, she floated away like a shadow, she was happy."

A few tears ran from the old man's dull eyes. He stopped for a while, he waited for the weeping that was stuck in his throat to pass. He was determined to finish his story:

"When I opened my eyes it was dawn. After riding my horse for a long time I reached a small fisherman's village. I crossed to the west of the Nile with a rowboat. In the thick fog, the high towers of Thebes Temple, and the huge silhouette of the granite statue of the Pharaoh could be seen. It wouldn't be right to go there. I wandered around listening to what people were talking about. A few days ago many palace servants, including women, had been burned to death. They were mentioning that one of the women was pardoned. Their only crime was believing in a single God that created all. My heart was beating wildly. I wanted to believe that the woman who was pardoned was Rispa. I was worried about my children and wanted to rejoin them at once. They were happy about the executions of the Israelites, they felt inauspiciously joyful about their deaths. 'Long live our god that gives us life, and abundance to our gardens. Those who didn't accept him as a deity deserved it,' they were saying. The words of the fishermen had annoyed me deeply. The Pharaoh's nation was irreligious and treacherous like their king. I buried my pain in my heart and started to wait for the night.

When dark fell I followed the Nile and walked to the south. I was cursing them all. I proceeded to the point exactly across from the village of my best friend Imran and his wife Yuhayil. They must have known what had happened. I hadn't lost my hope that my wife was one of the pardoned women. The Pharaoh must have spared her life but dismissed her from the palace. In that case the only place she could take refuge was the home of Yuhayil. Then I searched for a narrow part of the Nile where the current wasn't strong. I knew such a place a little further on. It was pitch dark everywhere. I lowered myself into the cool water of the Nile and started to swim. There weren't any crocodiles in this area, but I was still doubtful. However the desire to rejoin my wife and children gave me strength. Imran's house was very close to the shore, when I reached the riverside I started to run towards his adobe cottage. The dogs of the village were barking excitedly.

I had almost reached his garden when the door of the cottage opened. Imran appeared with a big torch in his hand, he was trying to understand why the dogs were barking. He almost fainted when he saw me right in front of him. Then he started to tremble as if he had come down with malaria. 'What's wrong, are you seeing me for the first time?' I yelled, he wasn't hearing me, he was only trembling. 'There's nothing to worry about, I'm alive.' I shouted. He couldn't recover. The shadow of Yuhayil appeared at the door, she had Aaron in her arms. When she noticed me she screamed terribly. I was surprised. What was going on? She let Aaron down as if dropping him. I came to my senses with the weeping of Imran and his wife, they had burst out crying."

"That's enough Father!"

Abel's commanding voice had dropped like a bomb in the room:

"Who knows how many times we have heard these painful memories from you. You are wrecking yourself and us too."

His voice softened all of a sudden:

"Please father, do not upset our guests any further with these painful memories. You can see that they are tired and sleepless."

The old man didn't seem to hear his son's voice:

"I understood that Rispa had died, I started to weep with them. I do not remember how much time had passed. When I pulled myself together, I murmured 'They had no pity for her, did they?' They only nodded. My beloved wife had died, suffering who knows how much pain among terrible flames. My wings were broken, my world was dark, and everything had ended for me. We were all hugging, as if we were a single body."

The trembling flames of the torches had grown dim, the room had got a little darker. Abel was almost begging:

"Please father, don't you hear me?"

Ezekiel was determined to finish his story:

"Abel caught my eye, he was sleeping on the low sofa on the other side of the room like an angel. 'How about my children, them?' I wailed. My babies had burned to ashes in wild flames, just like their mother."

The old man had finished his story, and burst out crying. Abel was also crying for his mother and his siblings who were burned twenty six years ago by the Pharaoh's order. Sinuha had frozen, he was petrified. He had never desired to kill the Pharaoh so much. He looked at his friend, Moses was crying too. Tears running from his eyes were wetting his cheeks and running towards his neck.

Now he was sure that he wouldn't get upset with him because of his hate of Ramesses.

The Poor Things Were Being Torn to Pieces by Hungry Animals among Screeches

othing but the weeping of the father and son could be heard in the room. The old man was facing his past once again, what he couldn't forget the most was Abigail and her innocent face. All of a sudden he remembered the nightmare he saw at the king's graveyard. He could almost hear his little baby crying out 'Save me daddy, save me!' with her tiny lips. He couldn't forget that image. The old man wiped his eyes with the back of his hand and continued:

"That day, the Pharaoh returned from inspection early, and when he found out that I was missing he confronted the Queen. 'Ezekiel was close to my father, he was the palace carpenter. How can he not accept me who created the universe as a deity, how can he not believe in me? How can a servant that I gave food to worship the God of Joseph who was of the Hyksos, the God of my forefather's enemy Abraham.' he said and screamed madly. 'I shall not forgive him or his wife. Does he think he can escape the Pharaoh? I shall make him feel such pain that he will never be able to forget it as long as he lives.' he roared. Then he ordered: 'Throw the children into the fire with their mother.'

The innocent children went to the place they were going to be burned happily, they thought it was all a game. They stood next to their mother and started to wait. Even when the piles of hay surrounding them were lit, they didn't understand what was happening. When they were encircled by flames, they screamed terribly asking for their mother's help, but their mother couldn't save my babies either. They died in pain as their countrymen who shared the same fate. The poor bodies of live torches burned until they were black. Tiny Abigail's soft and tender body had turned black. They found her as a small lump of bones.

The Pharaoh and his vile vizier were celebrating this terrible scene by drinking wine, watching poor people die in laughter. At one stage he looked at Rispa. She was screaming out 'O Allah, there is no god but you.' till her last moment."

The silence in the room was spoiled by a loud noise. As if a heavy rock had fallen on the roof. The old man frowned and went quiet. The storm had got violent again. The window sashes were banging, roof boards were being ripped off and hurled around. The small room went white, and then deafening thunder was heard. The downpour was whipping the walls. The sounds of animals could be heard from the garden, dog barking was mixing with cow mooing.

Sinuha shivered. However this time he hadn't taken refuge in Amun, he had turned his heart to the God of Joseph again.

Abel went out to bring drinks; their mouths had gone dry. Moses looked at the old man with tears in his eyes. He was preparing to listen to the end of the story with an impatient curiosity. Abel entered the room with a tray full of fruit, turned to his father and said:

"The chimney has fallen down."

The old man paid no attention. He was under the influence of the storm within him. Moses couldn't stop the storm that the old man had started in his soul. He had been quiet for years and years. He believed tonight was the time to tell all he knew, even if it was going to end with death.

He was thin, very thin. His skin had wrinkled to the shape of his bones, clinging tightly to his body. His chest rose a few times. He started again with a quiet voice as if he wanted to use his voice efficiently:

"The Pharaoh was right, he had condemned me to a lifelong pain. For a while I hid in Imran's rowboat that he would go fishing in every once in a while which was in his garden on the shore of the Nile. However, after a while I was sure that the Pharaoh wasn't searching for me. For it wouldn't be hard to find me if he wanted to. He wanted me to suffer like that. Even though I knew he was well protected, I made plans to kill him for days, of course it was not possible. One night I saw a very strange dream in the rowboat tied to the shore. My ancestor Joseph told me how he was thrown in to a well by his brothers, and how he suffered, but he had been patient. 'Take refuge in Allah with patience.' he said. At that moment I noticed Abigail. O my God, how beautiful she was. Next to that Holy Prophet, she was smiling with love and happiness. Then Prophet Joseph pointed somewhere. When I looked there, I saw a great crowd passing to the other side of the Red Sea. I could almost feel the existence of Rispa, Ahinum and Kiledo among them. A large man wrapped in white clothes was leading them with a long staff in his hand. I couldn't see his face because they were very far away. However I woke up happily. I could still feel pain in my heart but I wasn't sad; I had seen them in heaven in the company of Prophet Joseph. I was going to be patient, whoever would control themselves, Allah would give them success in patience. As my Prophet had indicated, I took refuge in Allah when I was troubled, I decided not to run away. I was finding consolation in hugging Abel. I was seeing myself in my dreams helping the person that was going to save the Israelites from tyranny and take Prophet Joseph's holy body from here, and I was waking up excited. 'O my Lord, allow me to help that person.' I was praying.

Sinuha couldn't wait any longer, he jumped up in excitement:

"What did he look like, didn't you see his face?" he shouted.

"I don't know. Even though I've seen him many times, I could not remember his face when I woke up. I don't want to die without waging war in his army against the Pharaoh."

Excited, Sinuha said:

"Me too."

Ezekiel smiled:

"You are brave and honest like your father."

Then he turned to Moses and said:

"You too, young man."

After waiting for a while:

"The disasters for the Israelites weren't limited to this, new tortures were awaiting us."

Excited again, Sinuha said:

"What else?"

The old man smiled bitterly:

"Egypt had become very rich, starting with the nobles, everyone had started to live in luxury. Prostitution was increasing. The condition had affected the public too, women weren't having babies anymore. A baby was a responsibility, a burden, a handicap for pleasure and fun. However, the Israelites were increasing in numbers despite all the pressure.

Listen young men, Allah never forgets those who believe in him. But the trial was continuing, our patience was being measured. In time we adapted ourselves, we decorated our cottages with statues of the Pharaoh, big and small. However we weren't letting him into our hearts. We had understood the sly plans of the Pharaoh to abolish religious people, and were changing tactics to survive. The Pharaoh's regime was aware that our increase in numbers was a threat to their future, however they couldn't expel us either. For we had become a mass more than hundreds of thousands. If they were to do such a thing we could join forces with the Hittites or the Amurru's who were always at war with the Pharaoh, and add more to Egypt's distress. That's why he wanted to omit this potential danger that didn't accept his claim of being a god. In order to systematically commit genocide he started vile applications. He wanted to make the Israelites work in the hardest and most dangerous jobs, and annihilate those who didn't obey his orders with relentless tortures by burning them or throwing them to crocodiles. Finally he gave another of his tyrannous orders. The baby boys of the Israelites were to be killed as soon as they were born. Therefore, by decreasing the number of men they were going to prevent us increasing in numbers, we would weaken and not be able to revolt against him."

"Father, wouldn't you let our young guests sleep. Tomorrow will be a long day for them, they will go to the garrison early in the morning."

Abel wasn't really considering the young men. He was aware that the Egyptian princes were listening to the old man without blinking an eye, with great curiosity, and without any sign of impatience. It was what his father was telling that scared him. He was worried about what could happen to them. They had gone to a lot of trouble to cover their tracks. They had gone through a lot to own this little garden on the shore of the Red Sea. Everything could be ruined in a trice. If they were princes from the Pharaoh's family, it was impossible for them to leave Memphis alone or be abandoned in the middle of the desert without protection. How could the Pharaoh leave his own child in the desert for a whole day alone? There must be something going on. He had to get rid of them first thing in the morning before they got in trouble. The young men did look like honest people, but he shouldn't trust them so much. It couldn't be right to tell the tyranny the Pharaoh had done, to his own children. Yes, his father had suffered a lot, he knew this well but:

"Abel, be quiet and listen to me."

The old man's voice was so strong for the first time. As if a new strength had come to the old man's body.

Moses and Sinuha glanced at each other. They didn't want this speech to end. With the information they gained that night, many things on their minds fell into place. Unaware, they both looked at Abel as if to say "Why are you trying to stop him talking?" He had understood that he couldn't stop his father. With a voice that nobody could hear he murmured "Let's see what's going to happen," and started to wait to see how it would end.

The storm outside was continuing with the same fierceness, every now and then the roaring of the wind trying to rip the cottage out of the ground could be heard. The old man sat up in his armchair and started to continue at the same tempo:

"The Pharaoh's order was announced all over the country. The pregnant women of the Israelites were to advise the District authorities of their pregnancy without delay. Their husbands and even their neighbors were being held responsible for it, it was announced that hiding such a thing was a cause for death. Spies were put on the tails of pregnant women who followed them until birth, and after birth they would take note of the child's sex. Women's days were counted carefully, and Egyptian midwives would certainly be present at births too. The order given to midwives was clear. If the child born was a boy, he was to be killed immediately, if it was a girl, she was to be left alive. A great massacre had started. There was no mercy for these poor babies that had committed no offense other than being an Israelite. This terrible tyranny continued for a long time despite the lamentation of the mothers. There was a chief midwife named Shiphrah, who was a palace inspector. The felonious woman would seek out midwives who didn't follow the Pharaoh's vile applications and punish them violently. The child killers killed thousands of our babies before they even saw the world. Many puerperal women went crazy from the shock they went through, and some of them committed suicide. Those who tried to hide their new born babies from the government were sentenced to death as a family. Along with the hidden baby, the whole family would be thrown into the crocodile pools in Memphis. Hungry animals were tearing the poor things to pieces among petrifying screeches. Nobody could stop the Pharaoh or Haman, the Israelites were being submitted to the most vicious genocide.

They Were Being Castrated under the Sharp Knives of Midwives

All of a sudden the lounge went white. Then the ground shook with great noise. Everyone but the old man shivered and jumped up. The rumbling of the earsplitting noise weakened as it spread in waves. The terrible crackling noise that could be heard from a breaking tree was heard from the garden.

Abel was trembling, he couldn't think what he should do. Stutteringly:

"Lightning must have struck," he murmured.

It was as if the old man hadn't heard anything:

"Even women who picked cotton in fields couldn't escape this disaster. The men of the Israelites who carried rocks that would crush their necks in the mountains, who laid adobe and bricks were praying to their Lord for their babies to be girls. That was the only way to avoid the grief of losing a child. Allah was our only refuge. We had all clearly understood that true fear was being away from his refuge."

Sinuha interrupted:

"It is said that the Pharaoh did so because of a dream he had."

"Possibly. However, I had heard that it was advised by oracles personally to Ramesses. But the true reason for killing the baby boys of the Israelites was to change the population increase in favor of the Copts."

"Do you think that is the only reason?"

"Our ancestor Prophet Abraham is well known by Egyptian rulers, moreover, the thought that Allah will send Prophets from his lineage scares them even centuries later. The doubt that someone among the Israelites will dethrone the Pharaoh and destroy Egypt is always on their minds. This concern is alive in their hearts."

"Is the future of Egypt to be saved by killing babies?"

"They must have thought so. However, the real cause of disaster is tyranny and evil getting out of hand."

"Evil is everywhere."

"When tyranny gets out of hand, nobody can prevent the possible disasters. For, in such conditions the Hand of Power intervenes directly. It holds the hands of those who were wrongly done by. Brings good people together and makes them brothers and sisters. Our nights were so dark, and the darkest night's morning would be early."

"What happened then?"

"The pressure from the royals increased, because in the near future it was going to be impossible to find workers for their fields. When your father's efforts were added to this, the Pharaoh had to take a step back. Killing baby boys was reduced to only every second year."

Sinuha was happy. His thoughts about his father were being confirmed for the first time by a stranger.

"However our ordeal wasn't over. New tortures were awaiting our babies that they didn't kill. Now they were losing their manhood under the sharp knives of midwives. Felonious midwives were allegedly treating baby boys by tying their testicles from behind to prevent them dying from hemorrhage, then removing one after the other, and cauterizing the veins. That is, as our babies' lives were being spared, their manhood was taken away, thus, they were trying to prevent our lineage increasing in numbers."

"What a horrible thing."

"It couldn't be said that these operations were successful. Most of the babies were dying during this torture. Slitting their throat hadn't completely stopped of course. Some blood thirsty midwives were slyly continuing doing it, and the officials weren't stopping them. Our babies' ordeal went on like this for years. Finally, Egyptians had found a solution for employment and our population increase. However fear doesn't stop things happening."

With great dignity Moses said:

"I had heard some of what you told from Queen Mother."

Excited, Sinuha said:

"Me too."

Moses:

"Queen Mother and the Pharaoh think differently on many matters. Do you have any idea about this?"

"Listen young men, Queen Neferure is not a Copt, she is a foreign princess of Amalika. She sacrificed herself for her country, married into the palace at the age of seventeen and became the Pharaoh's favorite. Her real name was Asiya. Her name comes from Asenath, the name of the wife of Prophet Joseph. Although idolatry was widespread among the people of Amalika and Mittani, there were also many people who believed in a single god. Asiya had hidden her faith in a single god, she hadn't let anyone know about her faith in Allah."

The princes were surprised. Moses couldn't stop himself and said:

"Thank God I was born from a mother who believes in Allah. At least one side of me isn't Copt."

"Listen to me carefully, for some of what I am about to tell, even my son doesn't know."

After a tired sigh, the old man started talking again:

"My friend Imran was a very self-sacrificing friend, he was closer to me than a brother. Working together we built a scrappy shack in the garden of his cottage, right next to the Nile. I was living there with Abel. Sometimes I would fix the villagers' chairs, and sometimes I would go cotton picking. I couldn't endanger Imran. I changed my name to Absalom. In case of a search being carried out I was going to take refuge in the Nile, hide among the reeds on the shore, and if necessary try to escape by swimming.

No hero can escape the arrows of fate.

Two years had passed since the terrible incident, nobody had come looking for me. When we were alone I would hug Abel and cry.

It was the year that baby boys were killed or castrated. Imran's wife Yuhayil was pregnant. We were in fear. We were begging to Allah every night, praying together for the baby to be a girl. However Yuhayil was saying that she had dreams, and that the baby was going to be a boy. Midwives that were touring the neighborhood examined her too, but something surprising happened. Her belly was so small that even though she was past five months pregnant they hadn't understood it. We were happy; because when the midwives came again the baby would have been born already. After four exciting months the baby was born, it was a boy. Yuhayil was very scared. She was afraid for her baby, the thought of its throat being slit was driving her crazy, she was living in frustration from the thought of losing her baby. None of us had come up with a logical solution to save the baby's life. How could we stop it crying, how could we prevent it? A jealous neighbor's notification would be the end of all of us. They would kill us all without pity.

We thought for weeks to find a solution. Meanwhile the baby was 4 months old. Yuhayil would always breast-feed the baby under a quilt, and didn't know what to do when he cried. Surprisingly, the baby wouldn't cry, or if he did he would cry quietly like a grown up person, as if he could guess what could happen. The mother would go to the shack I had abandoned some nights and breast-feed the baby there. I had left Abel with my sister in Karnak a while ago, and Imran had sent Aaron to his relatives far away. Only the twelve year old daughter Miriam was at home. She was a scrawny thin girl.

Yuhayil's fears had become obsessive. She didn't want to leave the baby for a single moment, because the midwives' inspection days were near. On those inauspicious days, the spies that came with the midwives would look under every rock. One night, as usual, we were talking about what we could do with Imran. All of a sudden Yuhayil came in. She was shaking and crying, tears were running down her cheeks. Her face was red. We understood that she had woken up from a terrible nightmare. 'Without me having a chance to open it, our door was broken open with a great noise' she murmured. 'Then people with dark faces filled the room, it was obvious they were people from the palace. Midwife Shiphrah was among them too. She grabbed my baby from my arms and knocked me over. Taking no notice at all of my screaming she cut the baby's throat in a single move. Everywhere was red from the blood that squirted from the hair like veins in his neck. I was losing my mind, screaming like crazy. I jumped on Shiphrah at once, I woke up as I was trying to strangle her. And I saw my beautiful baby was sleeping soundly next to me. I hugged him tightly, I kissed and smelled him. I cannot stand being parted with my baby Ezekiel, I will die.' Her tears were pouring out of her eyes. 'My heart is fluttering like a bird with the fear of losing my baby, I am constantly crying for its misfortune.' Wiping her eyes with the back of her hands, 'A little while ago I was half asleep. I was startled by a deep voice, but there was nobody around. That strong but not scary voice said to me: "Continue to breastfeed your baby. When you are afraid of him being harmed, put him in a crate and leave him to the Nile. Do not be afraid or sad, you will be reunited. We will give him back to you."

Imran and I looked at each other. Divine Power was intervening, coming to help the trembling mother. It had inspired her what to do, how to act. The baby would be in its guardianship in the Nile. It was turning the river into a refuge, and the water into a bed. Neither the tyrant Pharaoh, nor his oppressing accomplices could reach that perfect refuge under protection of Divine Power. The Divine voice had said that the baby would be given back to her. In that case there was no need for us to worry about the baby's life, or be sad because we weren't by its side. This inspiration was like an oasis' coolness in the desert for Yuhayil's heart.

Her eyes looking for pity were locked on me. Since the baby was going to be left to the Nile, it was my duty to make a crate to protect it from the water. These two self-sacrificing people had taken many risks for me, helped me through hard times, and hidden me in their house at the risk of death. Now it was my turn, I was going to help them.

I was a carpenter, I obtained the materials without drawing the neighbors' attention. I bought cedar wood which was water resistant, enough tar to fill in between, and a lock. In the night I would go to my shack on the shore of the Nile, and work trying not to make noise. Meanwhile the baby had become 8 months old. Two weeks later I had managed to build a small boat that was almost a meter long. To prevent it taking on water I covered its inside and outside properly with tar. And for it not to overturn I placed weights at the bottom of it and tested it again and again. To protect the little baby from the snakes and crocodiles in the Nile, I covered the small boat with a hatch, and turned it into a crate. And of course I didn't fail to open small holes on top of it so that the baby wouldn't suffocate. I also added a lock so that the baby couldn't lift the hatch and fall in the water. I made the inside of the boat a comfortable cradle for the baby. This little boat was both safe and cute. Imran and his wife both liked the crate very much.

We were hearing that the inspections were getting stricter and stricter. Yuhayil had spread out a soft bed for the baby to sleep soundly in the boat. The small boat that I had tied to the shore with flax rope was ready to sail. Whenever Yuhayil saw anyone suspicious she would put the baby in the crate and leave it to the Nile.

Moses, You Are the Son of Imran

*I*t was a hot summer night. Because it was very dark we had lit the torches and were eating our dinner which consisted of boiled cracked wheat. The door of the cottage was being knocked on as if it was going to break. A voice could be heard shrieking "In the name of the Pharaoh!" We didn't know what to do. Miriam ran to the door, Yuhayil ran to the garden. As we opened the door the emperor's soldiers filled the room. They were searching everywhere, yelling "It's not here," in anger. Imran and I were watching them from the corner we had crouched in. A young officer gave the order "Quick, search the garden too." Soldiers with torches started from my shack and searched the whole garden bit by bit. They were poking everywhere with their spears, under the trees, the reeds on the shore of the Nile, everywhere they were suspicious of.

Yuhayil had crouched on the spot and was shaking as if she had malaria. We were holding our breath, waiting for this nightmare to end. It took more than an hour for them to search that little house. The young officer turned to Shiphrah who was looking at us full of hate and said "There's no baby here." The chief midwife didn't speak for a long while, she was gazing at Imran with suspicious eyes. Then, all of a sudden she said "Let's go." We were safe.

With the door closing Yuhayil collapsed, she had fainted. She didn't recover easily. A little later when she pulled herself together, she looked at us with tired eyes, and talked wearily: 'I abandoned my baby. I abandoned my baby. I ran to the crate and cut the rope. I abandoned him to the Nile, to those wild currents, I abandoned him.' She burst into tears, another malaria attack had started. We were too confused and tired to say anything. With a mysterious incentive we hugged each other and started to cry out loud. All our hope was in Allah's promise, and the Divine Power that wanted us to leave it into the water in a crate.

Yuhayil stopped crying all of a sudden. Turning to her daughter she said "Run Miriam, follow the trace of my son." As soon as the little girl heard the order she ran out of the cottage like lightning and disappeared in the dark. It was as if Imran's wife had lost her mind, she was looking at us with dull eyes, continuously murmuring "I abandoned my son." I was afraid that her bellowing would be heard by the neighbors. 'I did something that a mother should never do. I abandoned my baby to the water with my own hands. How could I do this? How did I seek his rescue in this river's wild waters? I sent my darling to death with my own hands. Why did I believe that weird voice?' she said, repeating her regrets one after the other. She went quiet for a while, she didn't say anything. Then she started to repent. 'Forgive me Allah, what am I saying?' she murmured. Thankfully she had come to her senses. Rising her hands to the sky 'Allah, I will be patient with your trial' she said. She had found peace.

The morning had come but Miriam hadn't returned yet. What had happened to the little boat and its passenger? Had the crate endured the wild waves of the Nile? Was the baby alive, or had it been torn to pieces by a hungry predator? Where was the tiny baby, where was he? As someone who knew the grief of losing a child, I could understand the fire in their hearts.

It was almost midday when the door was knocked loudly, it was Miriam. Trying to catch her breath, she started to tell what happened: 'I took a shortcut to the small bay ahead. I started to wait for my brother to arrive there. The sun had risen. A little later I saw the crate floating along on the water. There were workers in the fields. I followed the crate without them noticing me. The Pharaoh's summerhouse could be seen ahead."

Miriam stopped for a short while, her excitement was obvious. Then with a great effort she gave us the news that terrified us all:

"My brother went to the Pharaoh's palace." She kept on repeating it.

Yuhayil collapsed on the spot. She passed out murmuring "It promised me, my child was going to be safe."

The young princes were curiously waiting for the end of this story. Sinuha couldn't help asking:

"What happened to the baby?"

"That day a friend of mine who worked in the palace said that I was being searched for. After advising Imran and his wife to trust Allah's promise I took Abel and left the village. I went north without stopping, towards the Delta. My first stop was Faiyum Valley. I had heard that the Pharaoh had started work there to dry up the marsh. Workers were coming in from all over the country, even from neighboring countries. I joined the tens of thousands. I worked there for five years under the name of Absalom of Prut, nobody recognized me. Meanwhile Abel had grown up, he was a young man at the age of seventeen. I wrote a letter and invited Imran to my scrappy shack in the valley.

Less than a month later he came. He had lost weight, caved in, but he looked happy. Just like you, I was wondering about the tiny baby. He had been saved from death with the help of Queen Asiya. He told me things that were unbelievable. The tiny baby hadn't accepted to be breastfed for exactly eight days, he had withstood hunger. Criers had been sent out to find a wet nurse. Finally Yuhayil heard of it too, and applied to be the wet nurse of course. That is, the baby's real mother entered the palace as a wet nurse and breastfed her baby."

Moses' eyes had opened in amazement, turning to Sinuha he said:

"How surprising, isn't it?"

Ezekiel was smiling:

"Be patient and listen."

Abel interrupted:

"You never mentioned this to me."

"They called the baby Moses, by bringing together the Coptic syllables 'mo', which meant water, and 'ses', which means tree. Because he had come from the Nile and the forest."

A deep silence took over the room, they weren't even breathing. The old man turned to Moses and said:

"You are that child son. You are the son of Imran, not the Pharaoh."

Moses had jumped up all of a sudden and sat back down again, a storm was brewing in his young heart. Could the words of this old man that he had just met a few hours ago be true? Or was he face to face with a lunatic or a poor senile? He thought about where and who he could get the truth from, how he could reach true information.

Abel was dumbstruck too, he stuttered:

"Father! Father! Are you aware of what you said?"

A faint pinkness was covering the room, it was the break of day. Their faces were brightened with the first rays of the sun. Moses had frozen, he wasn't moving at all. The meaningful look on his face was gone. Sinuha wasn't able to say the words of consolation words he had planned in his mind. Although he intended to talk a few times, he finally bowed his head and kept quiet.

With his softest voice Ezekiel tried to resolve his doubts:

"You can ask Queen Asiya about this, but the Pharaoh must not find out."

After waiting for a while:

"Allah delivered you to your enemy when you were helpless, and had no power at all, He raised you in his hands, in his palace. Who knows? Maybe you are the one that is going to save us from this tyranny."

* * *

Moses was excited. He wanted to get to know Imran and Yuhayil. The people who he thought were his family had changed overnight. He had to find out the truth right away. He couldn't wait to see the Queen, he had never liked the Pharaoh, and he had even hated him. After every incident he had wished not to be the son of this tyrant man. However, wishing something and coming face to face with it were two different things. He was thinking that he should be happy for this, he did feel joy, but he was also sad. He was aware that the Pharaoh didn't like him. Especially after his brother Minaptah was born, it was even more obvious. But Queen Mother was different.

He felt all alone for a moment. Were his real mother and father alive? How about his sister Miriam, and his brother Aaron? "So I am an Israelite, while my countrymen were struggling in tyranny I was living the good life in palaces," he murmured. However he couldn't deny that he had received a good education.

He didn't believe in Egyptian gods, he owed this to Asiya; now he felt even more indebted to her. She had taken him in to the palace from the Nile in his tiny crate, and saved him from absolute death. She had always loved him, and taught him the truth. He thought that those who really love don't expect anything in return. Who knows, maybe his real mother wouldn't have been so warm towards him. He thought he wasn't being fair to his mother he hadn't seen and may never see, his mind was mixed up.

He woke from the sleep he was in with the soft voice of the old man:

"Don't worry, the Pharaoh thinks you are the child of a poor Copt, but you should be careful."

Moses trusted this brave old man even more with every passing minute, the warmth in his heart for him was increasing. He felt indebted to him. Hadn't this suffering man made that tiny cradle that floated on the Nile for him?

Now he was happier than he was a few minutes ago:

"Is my family alive?"

"I don't know, I haven't heard of them for twenty years."

"Why?"

"The spies of the Pharaoh had found my trace, when I heard this I fled from Faiyum. The only thing that keeps me alive is my son Abel."

A bitter sorrow took over the old man's face:

"I don't even know if the Pharaoh did any evil to Imran or his family. With the money I saved in the valley I settled on this desolate shore of the Red Sea. I have been living here with my son and grandchildren for exactly twenty years. As a poor villager from Prut I grow fruit in my small garden, and breed animals. In fact I am so old that all I can do is worship Allah, and love my grandchildren too of course."

The sun had risen so bright that the room was sparkling. There was no sign of the storm that had started at midnight and continued nonstop through the night.

Abel affectionately said to his father:

"Please father, you must rest."

The old man was really very tired, he had spoken continuously throughout the night. With one last effort he said:

"There is eternity ahead of me to rest."

He turned to Moses again and said:

"I had seen you twenty four years ago as an eight month old baby. Yesterday you came out of the darkness. Now you are in front of me as a strong and smart young man standing tall. I thank Allah who sent you to me. Since

I was able to tell you the truth before dying, I don't care if I pay the price with my life.

Moses. I am very old and weak, I don't think I will see my nation leaving Egypt. I won't be in his army, I won't be able to support him. But I swear upon the force that saved you from the Nile, you carry a piece of him in your heart."

Tears of joy running from the old man's eyes were hardly making their way between the deep lines on his face slowly towards his chin:

"Come on, don't be late. The garrison isn't far away, only a few miles north. Abel will take you" he managed to say.

Moses woke up from the night of his life, full of surprises, grasped the dried up hands of the old man who was bent double in the corner, then hugging his weak body with affection:

"Do pray for me a lot" he said. And then added,

"Is there anything that you want to say? We might not see each other again."

"Give my best regards to Asiya, my dear Queen. She risked her life to save me, but I didn't have the chance to express my gratitude."

Then he turned to Sinuha:

"Tell your father that the crazy carpenter is alive."

The old man stood up leaning on his staff. As he was walking towards the door he said:

"Do you see how bright the sun is today? Don't ever cry for the setting sun, think about what you will do when it rises."

The young men watched the roaring waves of the Red Sea for a while. However it wasn't as appealing as it used to be to Moses.

O God of Joseph,
I Believe in You

The people of Thebes had taken to the roads to welcome the Pharaoh returning from the Nubia expedition. Along with the Coptic majority, there were also black slaves, full lipped Syrians, and even yellow haired Phoenicians moving along as corteges to watch the return of Ramesses. Priests wearing leopard skins were running around with miniature god statues in their hands.

* * *

The Agriculture Minister's carriage was for three. The front of it was protected by a semicircle barrier. It was made of bronze and decorated with red and green plates. The harnessed horses made those who saw them jealous. About twenty slaves ready to take orders any moment were right next to the carriage.

Smiling at his son with love, Imhotep said:

"How are you Sinuha, we haven't seen each other for a long time, but I have been informed of your success, and I am proud of you."

The minister's spectacular carriage was proceeding out of town among greenery decorated with palm trees, and as it moved away from Thebes it was surrounded by magnificent mansions and manors in flamboyant gardens. The magnificent palace of Ramesses with its towers reaching to the sky, the mansion of Haman on the west shore of the river, the manor of Korah with its garden decorated with lotus flowers were dazzling everyone. The Amun Temple on the horizon was blocking half the view with its gigantic structure.

As the minister's carriage pulled by well-groomed horses proceeded through this unique view Sinuha didn't look happy. When they reached the celebration grounds they saw that thousands of Egyptians had filled the square in colorful clothes. There was no room at all in the clearing that stretched as far as the eye could see. Only a small lane on the south road was trying to be kept open for the Pharaoh and his cortege. This narrow road was stretching to the city like a red rope.

The carriage of the Agriculture minister was placed in the spot reserved for it opposite the stand for nobles. Imhotep moved towards the steps, Sinuha was next to him too. The little Prince shook off his recent absent mindedness and started to look around the lodges in the stand with his Nile blue eyes. His eyes were scanning carefully, he was looking for the familiar face he believed would be there. Even though he looked through the part where the nobles were seated a few times, he couldn't see her. Because his father had focused on the south road, he hadn't noticed that Sinuha had clenched his fists in sorrow and hopelessness.

Even though the sun had turned to the west the scorching heat hadn't decreased, not the slightest breeze could be felt in the air. As if a terrible giant from a story had blown its hot breath over the desert. All of a sudden an awesome murmuring rose from mouths filling the clearing, heads turned to the south. The Imperial infantry was coming. A yellow cloud of dust covered the sky. The calibrated steps were getting closer. Finally the horn and drum band appeared through the yellow mist all of a sudden. An unbearable noise overtook the clearing. The horn players were playing a victory anthem with their shiny horns. All of these celebrations were to welcome Amun's shadow on earth. This could be considered insufficient for Ramesses whose huge statues could be found on every street corner.

After the horn and drum band, the black slaves were seen. With their uncovered heads and bare feet, only wearing striped cloth beneath their waists, the poor things were wretched. Some of them had been tied from behind by their arms at their elbows level. Some of them were even tied to each other's neck. They had been walked savagely for days in pain. Those who collapsed from fatigue or sunstroke were whipped so that they would get up, if they refused to stand up, or they couldn't, their head was chopped off with a single blow of a sword on the spot.

Their countrymen who approached to help were whipped wildly, not even being allowed to look at them with pity. Their crimes unknown, some young men were wearing iron shackles on their ankles, and some were carrying heavy planks tied to their backs. They were treated like wild animals, the poor things were racked with pain.

The lucky ones of these poor slaves that had been torn from their homeland would serve in palaces of the Pharaoh, Haman, or other nobles. But without any doubt, most of them were candidates to break rocks in Hammamat Valley. They would share the same painful fate with the Israelites.

After the male slaves, the women and young girls group was seen. They were walking in tattered covers. Some women had tied their tiny babies to their necks with dirty clothes. The beautiful ones would be given to the service of palaces, but most of them would be sent to the cotton fields.

The spoils of war weren't limited to slaves. Trunks full of gold dust, ivory, ostrich feathers and beautiful fragrances were being carried by these slaves. Also, hundreds of wild animals had been captured and put in strong cages made of tree branches.

When the slaves had ended, hundreds of flags decorated with god figures were seen. The flag with a crocodile pattern on it symbolized Sobek, the god pictured as a cow symbolized Hathor, and the god designed as a cat symbolized Pakhet. The magicians and priests who saw the flags bowed so far to hail their gods that their noses were going to touch the sand, some of them were throwing themselves flat on their faces.

Finally, the Pharaoh came into view. The nuns were sprinkling beautiful fragrances on him, throwing rose petals, and then without turning their backs they were moving back step by step. A nauseating smell of rose began to flutter in the scorching air. The Pharaoh was sitting on a throne with lion legs, the throne was carried on the shoulders of eight high ranked commanders. Ubiante, the commander of cavalry, could easily be noticed at the front with his shapely face and strong muscles. His strong body was shining under the sun because of sweat, he looked like a bronze statue.

The throne was gold gilded all over. The emerald, coral and ruby ornaments on it were giving off different colors with every move of the throne, sparkling colorful lights like a rainbow.

Four huge black slaves escorting the throne were swaying the long semicircle shaped feather fans slowly, trying to cool their Pharaoh sitting in his throne as cold as a statue without moving at all. The conceited king was sitting up straight, with his hands on his legs, just like an idol, looking around arrogantly. A helmet covered in shiny stones on his head, and a ten row necklace again made of precious stones on his chest, were attracting attention. His top wasn't covered. His lower body was wrapped in thin cloth that was very precious. His skirt full of rich creases was being held by a finely engraved gold belt.

A large lion was lying at the Pharaoh's feet. The tamed animal was sitting, puffing up its mane which made it look bigger than it was, stretching out its strong claws magnificently, careless of what was going on around it.

When the chariots of the cavalry units appeared Sinuha leaned over to his father and murmured something. At the end he said:

"I'm going."

The young Prince left the stand without waiting for his father's answer. He turned his eyes to the lodge where Tiye could be for the last time, but he couldn't see her once again. His lips twisted in pain. What could have happened? Why hadn't she come to the ceremony? Who could dare to be so disrespectful not to welcome the Pharaoh, did she have a death wish? Being the daughter of Haman didn't give her this right. He walked down the stairs of the stand with fast steps, not knowing what to do.

When the Pharaoh had reached his fancy palace, passed through long corridors where pillars decorated with hieroglyph were lined up and entered the throne lounge, Sinuha had come to the end of the road heading to the city and reached Tiye's mansion. Haman must have been with Ramesses, all of Egypt was busy with him now. Nobody but black slaves here and there could be seen in the streets. Ezekiel's story came to his mind. "Poor Moses", he said to himself. His hate of his uncle made his face darken even more.

Even though he was an Egyptian and dressed like an Egyptian, people who saw Sinuha couldn't believe they were from the same origin. With his yellow hair, round white face and thin lips he was very different from the Copts. His eyes weren't black like Egyptians, they were Nile blue.

Taking every risk for Tiye, Sinuha thumped hard on the door of the mansion and shouted:

"Is there anybody home?"

A little later, approaching footsteps were heard. The door opened squeaking slowly and a large black head stuck out. The black slave bent over with great respect and said:

"Yes my noble sir."

The young Prince tried to pull himself together and asked:

"Where is the princess?"

"Far away sir."

Sinuha was shocked, he turned pale. Stutteringly:

"What... Where did she go, where could she go?"

"I don't know, noble sir."

"Tesi. Where is Tesi?"

"She went with her sir."

"When?"

"A few days ago."

"When will they return?"

"My grand master said that they wouldn't return."

Sinuha broke down, he felt dizzy all of a sudden, he held on to the wall with one hand. Her father had taken her away from him. His hate of Haman multiplied.

The black slave requested his permission to close the door. The redness of evening was falling on the horizon, the sun was slowly melting on the west side of town. Sinuha walked the streets of Thebes a few times in pain. He felt very bad, and wanted to wreck everything.

They had returned to Thebes the previous day. Moses had set off with the royal boat for Karnak Palace where Neferure was; Sinuha had waved to him until the boat's fancy sail was out of sight. The young Prince was alone with his pain now, whereas he needed consolation so much. All of a sudden he thought of his friend's grief. His life had changed overnight, he had found out that he wasn't a noble of the Pharaoh's family but a child of an ordinary villager of the Israelites. Ramesses was not his father, neither was Neferure his mother. One had to have the willpower of Moses to overcome such a wrecking that struck like lightning into his life, he thought to himself. Realizing he didn't have half of his willpower he felt sorrow. There was no other way than to wait until the following day to talk to Moses.

With the pain settling in his heart he screamed:

"O God of Joseph, give me patience!"

He felt relieved. The voice inside him was telling him that he was getting closer to the God of Joseph each passing day. Who knows which corner of the country relentless Haman had sent his dear Tiye to? He was definitely going to trace her and find her, he wasn't going to turn over the girl he loved to the arms of Ubiante. With the solemnity of a wounded lion he headed to their mansion.

The Pharaoh came before his eyes, sitting in his gold gilded throne conceited, almost lost in colorful stones. And on the other side he thought of the slaves with shackles, the concubines walking barefoot on the hot sand, babies wrapped in dirty rags, and the bitter screams of Abigail when she was burning like a torch. He thought of the thousands of Moseses that were killed as soon as they were born. His hate of the Pharaoh and his treacherous vizier Haman overflowed from his soul. When he came to the door of their mansion he screamed:

"O God of Joseph, I only believe in you!"

He wasn't going to share his new faith with anyone but Moses.

The Baby That Didn't
Know Fire from Rubies

Queen Neferure's black hair with gold hairpins shining in it had been plaited finely, and thin tulle had been wrapped around it. A splendidly beautiful twelve row gold necklace was shining on her neck. Her intelligence could be seen in her black eyes, she was smiling affectionately. Her queen's crown was winking at everybody from the carved console, with red and blue stars sprinkled on its gold wires.

The sun was rising slowly, even though the large lounge windows were wide open, there was no movement in the pale blue tulle which was the same color as the walls. The palace on the shore of the Nile was very hot at that time of year.

Queen Mother sent out the black concubines that were trying to cool her down with camel hair fans. In her gold gilded armchair she was waving the fan in her hand fast, trying to cool down a bit. She spoke to Moses who was waiting quietly in the seat opposite her:

"Speak my child, I see you sad and out of spirits. They said that you wanted to see me, is there a problem?"

"I talked to Ezekiel."

"Who is Ezekiel?"

"You know, the famous carpenter of Thebes Palace."

Asiya's face clouded over, her fan had fallen in her lap. Distress appeared in her black eyes.

Moses went on:

"He told me everything. How he was saved, the calamitous death of his wife and children, and how he lived for years hiding out."

The queen's eyes were moving fast:

"What else?" she asked.

"And many other things."

After pausing for a moment, Moses said:

"That I am not the son of the Pharaoh, and that I came to the palace in a crate floating on the Nile."

Asiya was frozen. She was looking at Moses in sorrow mixed with amazement, and she couldn't speak. She was frozen just like a statue. Moses was continuing without stopping:

"How he made that tiny boat years ago, the story of the cradle he placed in it."

The Queen was hearing about Ezekiel's involvement in the crate for the first time. She felt depressed, her face had turned pale. After looking around in fear:

"That's enough, stop" she murmured.

Moses didn't stop.

"Dear mother, I was saved by you from certain death. I didn't suck milk for days, a wet nurse was sought for me. Finally my real mother was found, she breastfed me in the palace for months without revealing her identity. You named me Moses, the child that came from the Nile."

After a short hesitation Moses asked:

"I am an Israelite, aren't I?"

Asiya told him to stop once again, she was shocked. Twenty four years later, hearing the truth of which some parts she was hearing for the first time had tied her in knots. Her heart was beating wildly, and her body was shaking as if she had malaria. She couldn't stand it any longer. She closed her face with her hands and burst out crying. She cried for a long while without stopping. When she raised her head, her eyes were red. She slightly nodded her head as if to say "Yes." She wiped her tears with her lace handkerchief, she picked up the fan that had fallen on the floor. She had slightly recovered and started to talk:

"Listen son, I shall tell you everything from the beginning. I am the princess of Amalika, I married the Pharaoh for the love of my father who is a king. My father only believes in Allah, and accepts Joseph as a Prophet. That's why they named me Asenath, it was the name of the Prophet's wife. My father called me by the name Asiya. Because the Pharaoh was an enemy of Allah's Prophets, he changed my name to Egyptian, and made it Neferure."

After taking a deep breath:

"We had been married for a year, and we hadn't had a baby yet. At that time the Pharaoh was a twenty two year old handsome young man. He would do anything I requested straight away. But he was relentless. I'm not sure if it was a dream or the influence of magicians, but he ordered all the baby boys of the Israelites to be killed. When Grand Vizier Haman and the others supported him it turned into a massacre. As you know, nobody can stop him. Imhotep and I struggled a lot to stop the murders, however we weren't successful. The felonious practices went on for years. Finally he eased his order by deciding to kill the baby boys every second year."

Moses was listening with great attention, engraving each and every word in the depth of his memory. After wiping her damp eyes with her silk lace handkerchief, Asiya dived back into her memories:

"It was a hot summer morning. I was watching the Nile from the balcony of the coast palace in Thebes with Ramesses. Hundreds of concubines were scattered along the coast that stretched as far as one could see, all working. All of a sudden we noticed a tiny boat drifting towards the coast. The concubines rushed and pulled the tiny boat ashore. They were amazed when they opened the hatch of the crate on the tiny boat. Because a cute baby was smiling at them. The girls brought the beautiful baby with its cradle to us. The Pharaoh was shocked when he saw the baby was a boy. 'How did this baby escape death?

Didn't I order baby boys to be killed this year? Bring Shiphrah to me right away.' he roared. He reprimanded the chief midwife who was brought into his presence a little later so badly that the treacherous woman started to shake like a leaf."

She took a deep breath, her face had taken on a harsh look:

"The Pharaoh held you out to Shiphrah and yelled 'Kill him immediately, do you understand?' You were so cute, such a chubby baby, I couldn't allow them to kill you. Tears were pouring out of my eyes. I grabbed you from his hands all of a sudden. Crying, I said 'Don't you see darling? This child is over a year old. Whereas you had ordered new born babies to be killed.'

As if a secret force was making me help you. 'Darling, he's very cute isn't he? How could he possibly harm anyone?' I said and smiled. Ramesses was quietly watching me with a frown on his face. Without saying a word he looked at you for a long while, and then he stared at me. He was trying to read my mind. I was praying to my Lord for Him to save you. I mustered up my courage and begged to him: 'Please pardon him, he will support you when he grows up.' When I saw he was still hesitating: 'Let's adopt him, and raise him in the palace.' I said.

The Pharaoh walked away without saying anything after dismissing Shiphrah who was standing in front of him terrified. The warmth of my love had softened his heart, and soothed his anger. If Allah wishes to, He can protect a weak person from a powerful and cruel person. You had been miraculously saved from the Pharaoh who feloniously killed the babies of the Israelites without pity, without anyone's assistance.

Oh my dear Moses! You were left in my arms like an angel on earth. A little later I called my maid of honor, after giving you to her, I ordered her to find a wet nurse immediately. Criers were sent out, but it was no good, you weren't breastfeeding from anyone. I was helpless, I was afraid you would die of hunger. Finally I explained the situation to the Pharaoh in tears, I begged for him to help. He got angry again. 'Let's get rid of him.' he shouted.

I barely managed to calm him down. He finally accepted to send criers to close villages and coastal towns. The news that a wet nurse was being sought for a baby of the palace was heard everywhere. Eight days had passed since you had come to the palace. Weirdly, even though you were hungry for days, you weren't crying or losing weight. One morning a small girl who said she lived on the coast came. She said that she could find a wet nurse and wanted to see you. I gave her permission. She touched you with sincere compassion. And then: 'I know a wet nurse who can breastfeed this baby' she said, and added: 'And the family won't make any mistakes in bringing up the child.'

The Pharaoh was suspicious, with an angry voice: 'What do you mean by saying they won't make any mistakes?' he asked.

'I mean they will wish the happiness of you and your queen, your majesty.'

The little girl came back in the afternoon with a thin woman who she said was her mother. You were full of joy, you couldn't stay still. After the Pharaoh looked over the woman carefully:

'Where is your baby?'

She gave an odd answer:

'I don't have a baby.'

The Pharaoh ripped her clothes all of a sudden, her breasts were dry. The Pharaoh who looked over the woman in astonishment roared in rage:

'There isn't a single drop of milk in your breasts, what will you give this baby? '

The thin woman begged:

'O mighty Pharaoh, we are a poor family. I need money a lot, allow me to try.' And then without taking any notice of the astonishment in my eyes she took you to her breast and started to breastfeed you. The Pharaoh screamed in fear:

'She must be a magician.'

A room in one of the outbuildings was given to the woman from Karnak. You were growing fast, but the Pharaoh just couldn't love you. Even though you were a tiny baby he was suspecting you, making out something from your every movement, and was puzzlingly keeping away from you. Because I had come to the palace from another country all eyes were on me, my love for you had begun to raise doubt."

In excitement, all of a sudden Moses asked:

"Queen Mother, I always loved you, and I always will. Are my mother and father alive?"

"Dear Moses, Ezekiel and his wife were simple hearted, honest and honorable people who believed in Allah, the only God. But the Pharaoh nearly lost his mind because of Ezekiel not accepting him as a god, not believing in him. As he didn't forgive him, he also relentlessly tyrannized his wife and children. I am glad he is alive. And about your mother; after watching the woman that breastfed you close up I had understood she was your real mother straight away."

"What do you mean?"

"I was a mother too, it could be told easily by the way she looked at you and hugged you. The Pharaoh had investigated and found out that she was of the Israelites. When you were two years old, and your breastfeeding days were over I called your mother and told her what I knew. She didn't deny what I said. And then suddenly she dropped down on her knees and said:

'My dear queen, I beg you for my child not to be hurt. First I trust Allah and then you' she cried. I told her that I would conceal her secret throughout my life, that you would be raised by my side with my love, and that she shouldn't be worried. I explained to her that the Pharaoh and his men were suspicious about her, and if she was to stay in the palace and keep on taking care of you the truth could be unveiled, and that could cause her death. I advised her to leave her village and even leave the country for your safety. I gave her family a great fortune so that they could leave Egypt. I think they went to the north, to Mittani. Otherwise, your life and theirs could have been endangered. I haven't heard of them since."

The tears running down Moses' cheeks were wetting the sides of the gold gilded sofa. Now he was crying for his family that he never saw and probably never was going to see.

Moses broke the long silence:

"Now what do you advise me to do, which path should I follow?"

"Now you have learned the truth about yourself Moses. These facts must be kept a secret between Sinuha and you, nobody else should hear about them. You must remain being the son of the Pharaoh. Along with Sinuha you successfully completed your education and returned. A bright future is awaiting both of you. Despite Haman's reaction, Sinuha will be given a position in the treasury, a decision hasn't been given for you yet.

Listen son, as I taught you, the Lord of the skies, the earth and all between is only Allah, He has no partner or counterpart. First Abraham, and then Isaac, Jacob and Joseph are all Prophets sent by Him, they are Messengers. Asking for the help of idols and statues, following them, is making them partners of Allah's power, and associating partners to Allah. This belief takes one to Hell.

Worshiping the Pharaoh is the same. As you can see, Ramesses placed his statues everywhere, denying Allah and announcing himself lord. The Israelites lost a lot through the Pharaoh's oppression, but they continued to believe in Allah and His Prophets.

Dear Moses, these words of mine must stay a secret. The Pharaoh's tyranny has decreased gradually, he doesn't interfere with the belief of the Israelites as long as they accept him as a god. Those who believe in Allah protect themselves from his tyranny by keeping a few small statues in their houses.

Listen my dear child, the capital will soon be moved to Memphis. I will try to have you commissioned to the neighborhood of the Israelites just outside of Memphis. I shall tell the Pharaoh to give you the duty of researching and reporting their religion. There you will find a chance to get to know your own nation. We shall make assessments at suitable times. Are you ready for such a mission?"

Moses nodded his head to say "Yes." Asiya winked at Moses:

"Let's go to Thebes tomorrow, and celebrate the Pharaoh's Nubia success."

"Dear mother, what do you think about Sinuha?"

"He is an honest and intelligent young man. He can take care of himself. I believe he will find the truth in a short time. You know he loves you, he will never harm you."

"I was thinking of leaving the palace, and Egypt, to go to places very far away. Talking with you comforted me."

"If you had done such a thing you would have left me in indefinable sorrow. You made the right decision by thinking of talking with me son. You must stay in Egypt and choose to be patient. Without any doubt, the power that oversees us has considered our future too. Tonight be hosted by black slaves in the Seti Mansion on the coast, rest there, recover. With the break of day we will go to Thebes, alright son?"

She looked at Moses with compassion:

"Listen Moses, the name of the little girl that brought your mother to the palace twenty four years ago, your sister, was Miriam, and your mother told me that your elder brother's name was Aaron."

He Prayed to His Lord until the Break of Day

Moses didn't sleep at all that night. He watched the brightness of the moon that was reflecting off the Nile, from the wooden balcony of the mansion. The darkness of the night had covered the wild flames of the sun like a thick curtain. A hot breeze that made the palm tree leaves move was starting. His sorrowful looks turned to the stars that were winking happily. By joining some make believe lines in the sky an affectionate face appeared. This familiar face smiling to him from among the stars was his mother. Using the same method he drew the images of first his father, then Miriam and Aaron. They smiled at him with love too, he felt his sorrow lighten.

He tried to combine what he had heard from Ezekiel and Asiya. He thought about his childhood sorrows which he couldn't remember anymore. He imagined the trouble his mother went to in order to hide him from the midwives of the Pharaoh, the tiny crate that Ezekiel secretly built in the garden to protect him, the dangerous and scary journey he made in the dark of the night on the waters of the Nile, his twelve year old sister running along the coast with thorns pricking her feet. He dreamed of the concubines working in the garden of the palace breaking the hatch of the crate, and taking him in his cradle to the Pharaoh, Asiya saving him from certain death by defending him at the risk of her own life. He murmured that Allah had taken Prophet Abraham and Joseph to unreachable positions through various tests. He remembered Ezekiel's words:

"In this world, great happiness can only be reached after great pain and disasters."

He started to think about who was really protecting him. It wasn't his mother or his father, not Ezekiel or Asiya. They were only instruments. He smiled all of a sudden, he was going to continue with his dreaming game. He saw himself playing on the balcony of the palace. He hit the Pharaoh on the head with the big stick in his hand as hard as he could. He looked at the red spot and the bump on his forehead. He realized that his fists had clenched unintentionally. He murmured "Well done." He laughed out loud, he had cheered up.

Suddenly he burst into tears. Could his being saved miraculously while tens of thousands of children had been killed by the Pharaoh be a coincidence? The Hand of Power had clearly intervened; challenging the Pharaoh, Haman, and their armies. Using all means available, they had followed the babies of the Israelites that would be born, put agents on their tails so not a single baby would get away, with the fear of losing their command. The Hand of Power had handed him over to them, helpless and powerless, without them going to any trouble. Holy power had wished to protect him in the palace of the furious and bloody dictator, therefore it was challenging the Pharaoh, who had announced himself a deity, in his own house.

Moses raised his hands to the sky decorated with stars:

"O Lord! Without any doubt, you gave me this life, and then protected me from death many times, brought me up in the Pharaoh's palace, what is the purpose of all this? O the ruler of the sky and earth, you are my owner in this world and the hereafter, give me knowledge, show me the secrets of your power."

Moses, was a young man, but he had matured. He prostrated, and didn't raise his head at all. He prayed to his Lord until the break of day. Crying, tearing his heart out, in a state of mind even he couldn't comprehend, he asked for knowledge and wisdom.

The sun hadn't risen yet. He slowly raised his head from prostration. He felt his soul reaching eternal satisfaction. He was feeling strange pleasures that he couldn't understand. All of a sudden, he seemed to hear a voice from down below: "O Moses. We gave you knowledge and wisdom. This is how we reward those who do righteous deeds."

The Cause of Disasters Is
Weakness of Faith

 oses was passing his days in the outskirts where the Israelites lived, with the excuse of preparing research reports. The area was full of simple houses made of granite, limestone or adobe. The streets weren't clean at all. Wooden shacks would turn into weird shapes that scared one in the dark of the night.

The Pharaoh had given up killing the babies of the Israelites. However, his tyranny was continuing, increasing the pressure on beliefs day after day. Egyptians were worshiping the Pharaoh and the Apis Bull, and the Israelites were being forced to believe in the same way too. The youth of the Israelites were changing their minds, unintentionally adopting Egyptian beliefs and customs under influence of the intense propaganda they were exposed to. The only factor that prevented the Israelites from worshiping Egyptian idols was being discriminated as second class citizens, being exposed to maltreatment. Their hatred of the Pharaoh prevented them from living like Egyptians. Therefore they wouldn't accept the Pharaoh as a deity, and they didn't worship the bull. But, it couldn't be said that they were interested in Prophet Abraham's Hanif[2] religion either. Both the years that had passed between their Prophet Joseph and their time, and the agonizing captivity they were caught in, weren't allowing them to practice their religion. They were eating, drinking, practicing magic, and living an addicted life just like Egyptians. By the rule that what isn't practiced will be forgotten, they had forgotten what they knew.

Prince Moses was known as the son of the Pharaoh, however the Israelites liked him. Because he would sometimes spend the night in an earthen hut or a simple shed, trying to get to know his nation in rooms that oozed light through their walls, talking about the unity of Allah.

* * *

It was a hot summer night. The windows were wide open. A few families had gathered in old Jubal's house. The small lamp on the table was enlightening the surroundings; clean plates neatly arranged on the shelf were catching the eye. The neighbors were sitting around the room on cushions that were filled with hay. There were even children about eight to ten years old among them.

---

[2] One who has a sincere, sound faith in God and worships God with purity of intention.

Looking at the silhouettes in front of him, Moses started to talk:

"Look around you, such different stamps can be seen on every flower, these stamps are particular to Allah who created all. Nobody else can do that. Allah is one, everything is His. Think about the miracle of life, many things are made from one, with it."

Moses was sometimes surprised by what he said himself, every morning he was waking up different from the previous night, he was witnessing his knowledge increasing. Without fearing the tyranny of the Pharaoh, he was using every chance to call his nation to the unity of Allah, and to invite them to Prophet Abraham's Hanif religion. The old people of the Israelites had started to see him as one of them.

* * *

The Pharaoh had been in Libya for a long time. He was waging war with the tribes there, trying to supply slaves. Grand Vizier Haman was taking advantage of his absence, and was busy increasing his profits of the copper mines. Prince Moses was talking with Queen Asiya frequently, he was mentioning what he was doing in the villages of the Israelites, sharing his thoughts.

* * *

The evening had come once again. The fields where mature wheat ears were ruffling could be seen beyond the endless gardens stretching behind the village. Men and women workers were bending and straightening up cropping the wheat. A threshing sledge pulled by strong oxen was separating wheat from their stem, threshing was being done a little further ahead. A large herd of cows appeared in the distance. Well-fed oxen and cows were impatient to get to their barn as soon as possible, they were pushing each other wildly. Moses smiled and looked at the animals rushing into the barns bellowing coarsely. He murmured "I'm surprised by people accepting these innocent animals as deities."

He had been wandering the outskirts of Memphis and villages of the Israelites for months. He had watched his nation's lifestyle, observed their conditions, and seen the youth getting close to the Egyptian religion. It wasn't going to be easy to put them on the true path.

Old Jubal approached him with a smile after closing the door of the barn firmly:

"My dear prince, the young ones are finishing their work, could you talk to us about Allah again this evening?"

After the sun set they gathered on the porch of the adobe house. The flickering flame of the torch was slightly lighting their faces. The old man quietly said:

"O son of the Pharaoh, you have a heart like gold, you are very different from your father. I have a question for you, we believe in the single Allah just like you, but we are in great agony, what is the reason for it?"

Moses answered the question with another question:

"What do you do to stop sheep that are going off limits?"

"We throw a stone."

Moses smiled:

"Sheep that are subjected to a stone thrown by the shepherd say 'We are under the command of this shepherd. He takes care of us better than we can; since he doesn't approve of this I shall turn back.' You should begin to act in accordance with His approval."

Moses started his lesson in the Name of Allah:

"None of us make our own bodies, we don't have the power to do so. Both mentally and physically we aren't capable of creating it. Others can't do it either. You can try if you wish. Let's see if you can make your tongue which is the center of many pleasures, or your eyes which see all the beauties of the world? You can't. In that case, do not associate partners to Allah, do not worship bulls or statues as the Egyptians do. Do not explain events with causes. Events are created by the invisible endless power behind them. Causes are only a curtain, devices created to protect the secrecy of trial."

"So, are we the cause of our own suffering?"

"Pray plenty to Allah, the creator of the sky and the earth. He definitely answers prayers of the desperate. Sometimes in respect of prayers the biggest things can obey the smallest things. For example, for the sake of the prayer of a heartbroken innocent on a broken piece of wood, the storm and rage of the sea begins to calm down. He who answers prayers is the ruler of all that has been created. He is the creator of everything."

Moses was surprised himself at how he had learned so much in such a short time and how he could expertly explain it in a manner that his nation could understand. He was choosing his words carefully, picking his examples meticulously. He wasn't insulting the Pharaoh or Egyptians, he was expressing his own belief, basing his interpretations on rules of thumb. He had concentrated on belief in Allah. He was sure that the disasters that his nation was going through were caused by weakness of belief.

He Had Promised, He Wasn't Going to Be Seen on Their Side

The Pharaoh had returned from Libya. Haman and Korah delayed their profitable work until Ramesses' next expedition. Moses' report about the Israelites was ready. He returned to Memphis, discussed it with Queen Asiya and finalized it. They planned the time to present it to the Pharaoh together.

He was ready for his next mission, but there was a surprise awaiting him. With the break of day he went to visit his friend Sinuha. As his Queen mother had said, he was now the deputy treasurer. After hugging him sincerely, without allowing him to say anything Sinuha quietly said:

"Haman had your every step in Goshen followed, and reported everything you did to the Pharaoh. Ramesses will accept and question you after he inspects the Ptah Barracks. He was very angry, you should be careful."

"I should have guessed he would have me followed. There is no importance in the report then. It's good that you told me, I'll be prepared."

Looking at his friend's eyes:

"You look troubled, or is it Tiye again?"

"Her father sent her away from Thebes. I had the whole country searched but her trace hasn't been found yet."

"You must be patient. Let's think about a solution together."

"I will definitely find her. Can you imagine what a person like this, who is so cruel to his own daughter, would do to me when he has a chance?"

Moses nodded his head as if to approve. Then he stood up all of a sudden and walked towards the door:

"If you'll excuse me, I'm going to town. I have to think about how I will defend myself."

"In this agonizing midday heat?"

"I have to go now."

As the young Prince was walking away from the palace with quick steps, the fancy guards he walked past saluted him with respect. Despite the striped cloth on his head, the heat was boiling his brain. As he was walking towards the city his mind was on his Goshen adventure. Actually he was happy, he had passed almost two years with his nation, heart to heart. He wasn't afraid for himself, but he was worried for Asiya.

The entire city was asleep. Nobody could be seen around, no open shops were catching the eye. In Memphis every midday was like this, in this infernal heat everybody would take siesta. His mouth had dried, if only he could drink a glass of water. With hope of finding an open shop he headed towards the market place. He could have come here in a royal carriage with glitter inlaid curtains. But he had taken a dislike to the palace, its splendor didn't interest him.

He slowly walked through the streets of Memphis which looked like a ghost town, and reached the market place. He seemed to hear a voice; he listened carefully. Because silence had taken over, even a whisper could be heard. He wasn't mistaken, the voice was coming from a little further ahead. First he couldn't understand what it was, but as he got closer to it, shouting and screaming were mixing with each other. First he walked faster, and then he started to run.

When he turned the corner he was shocked. Two half-naked men were fighting regardless of the burning heat. Even though they were breathless and in blood, sweat and tears, they were punching each other with great hatred. He recognized one of them right away. He was someone close to the Pharaoh, Fetun, the head cook of the palace. Sand was all over his sky blue silk skirt. The eyebrow of the one who was covered beneath his waist with a simple waist cloth had opened, his face was covered with blood. From the severity of the fight one of his sandals had been hurled a few steps away. The condition of the Israelite didn't look good at all. Moses ran to their side:

"Stop, I'm telling you to stop, break up."

The Israelite had rolled to the ground again with the strong punch of Fetun. Now the two naked bodies were rolling on the sand like lizards, sometimes Fetun, and sometimes the Israelite was getting on top. Finally the Copt ended up on top of his enemy and started to strangle him with a great grudge.

Moses shouted even louder than before:

"Fetun, I'm telling you to let him go!"

The sweaty Copt was intending to kill his enemy. With a severe head butt he gave his opponent's face a blood bath. The Israelite groaned in pain.

Moses, shouted again:

"That's enough, get off the man."

"O son of the Pharaoh! Go away, don't tell me what to do!"

The man resisting strangling on the ground whose face couldn't be seen from sand and blood growled with a croaky voice:

"Moses, help me!"

Moses was surprised by a slave saying his name openly.

"Fetun, don't you hear me?" he repeated.

Moses, who noticed the poor man's eyes lose focus, jumped on the Copt like a tiger. With his strong arms he squeezed his wrists like a clamp, and ripped him off the Israelite. Fetun was still resisting, swearing at Moses again and again. Finally he screamed:

"I will complain to god Pharaoh about you!"

The raging cook was pushing Moses who was trying to stop him, trying to hit his enemy, insulting him. The young Prince was keeping quiet, being patient, trying to prevent him with his strong arms. The man on the ground was half unconscious, but he finally managed to take strength from the ground and sit up on the sand bent double. His face had turned into a red ball of blood and sand.

The cook was seeing red. Taking advantage of Moses stopping for a moment, he kicked the poor man who was trying to recover in the face severely. The man screamed in pain and fell into the sand, he was lying flat. Fetun's last act had driven Moses crazy. He swung his right fist like a cannonball towards the Copt. The single punch was enough for the member of the palace, he fell on his back. The Israelite was watching it all from where he had fallen, in fear and astonishment, gratitude could be read in his eyes.

Moses' face was mixed up. He had come to the marketplace for a sip of water, not for a fight. He asked the poor man:

"Who are you?"

"I'm of the Joabs, my name is Samiri."

"Why did you two choose to fight in this infernal heat?"

Moses' eyes turned to Fetun, he was lying flat on his back. Without waiting for Samiri's answer he shouted:

"Get up you foolish man."

No answer came from Fetun.

The young Prince tried to lift up this big Copt by his arms, but he couldn't; he was dead.

Moses murmured in astonishment:

"I didn't mean to kill him."

The young prince hadn't done this on purpose, his only aim was to help this poor man. His eyes grew in fear, he put his head between his hands and started to cry:

"O Allah, what have I done, what have I done" he was repeating.

He was young and strong; emotional and short tempered. He was an enemy of the Pharaoh, and anything to do with him, but he never intended to kill anyone.

"I didn't want to kill him, I didn't" he murmured.

This was a result of momentary anger; anger was the breath of the devil. He was feeling remorse for what he had done, and was relating it to the devil's deception. He shook his head with great sorrow:

"This is completely the devil's deception. For he is a clear enemy that misleads one."

He turned to Samiri, but he wasn't there. He was gone already. How could an Israelite ask for the help of someone from the palace, a prince, to beat his Copt enemy? How could a slave ask for the Pharaoh's son to help him against one of the Pharaoh's men, was it possible? Moses was crying and thinking. Samiri had called out "Moses, help me!" How could a slave dare to address him like that? Could Samiri know that he was an Israelite, he didn't think so. Who could have told him that, how could such information reach someone ordinary like him?

Or was spending the past two years with them the reason? Was it spending his days in adobe houses and wooden sheds, spending the night on hay filled cushions with those helpless people, inviting them to Allah's unity? Had his compassion for his nation been interpreted as him not having any ties with the palace anymore? How could a slave that he had never seen before dare to address him with his name? His activities in Goshen must have been misunderstood. In that case there was no need to be surprised by Haman's intelligence. Trying to defend himself against the Pharaoh wasn't going to change anything. No wonder Sinuha said "I saw he was very angry."

There was still nobody around. He thought maybe Fetun had fainted. Yes, he must have fainted. How could such a strong man die with a single punch that wasn't even that hard? He leaned over and checked on him again, he checked his pulse. His head fell down again; the man wasn't alive. His tears wet the hot sand. "O Allah! I have wronged myself, I harmed myself, forgive me," he begged. Because he had killed someone not allowed to be killed, without a reason, this was a major crime.

He knelt down on his knees and begged for forgiveness again and again. He cried and cried. Minutes went by. Allah didn't leave the sincere appeal of Moses unanswered. He could feel that he was forgiven for the sincerity of his prayer. When the heat of a believer's inclination raises so much, he can feel his prayer reaching Allah.

When Moses felt his prayer was accepted his whole body started to shake. In return for all the benedictions He bestowed he said:

"O Mighty Allah! I swear upon the benedictions You have bestowed upon us that I will not help criminals."

He had great advantages because he was from the palace. However he had learned something new from this fight. Even though his heart was not with the Pharaoh or his men, being referred to as his son put him in an associate position. A little while ago Fetun had said "O son of the Pharaoh!" to him. He didn't like being referred to with that title at all. He had understood that this was a trial to put a distance between him and the Pharaoh and his men. In a storm of excitement he made a promise to his Lord. He wasn't going to be seen on their side again.

He Believed He Would Be
Protected by Divine Power

obody had seen him, however he wasn't considering returning to the palace. After looking at Fetun's face which had turned to a beeswax color one last time, he headed out of the city.

He walked, walked and walked. He had been walking for hours. He was tired and worn out, he was breathing flames. He wandered around until the night fell. He didn't know who or what he was running from. As the sun was sinking in the sand he had reached a shack, he was desperate. He leaned his back on the shack and rested for a while.

He waited there until colors turned to gray. Then the dark took over, stars began to shine. He was excited like in Seti's palace.

"What kind of a night is this" he murmured to himself.

All of a sudden, he heard footsteps approaching, he couldn't stay there. He slowly got up, but his feet couldn't carry his tired body, he sat down again. He had taken his glitter inlaid sandals off his feet which had swollen from the heat a long time ago. He needed to sleep a bit, to recover. The footsteps had got close. He thought the guards had come to take him. He had to run, he ran away staggering. A little later the sounds stopped.

In the brightness of the moonlight he noticed a hill made of hay stacks. A little further ahead an adobe village house could be seen. Confused, hopeless and in fear, trying to think what he should do he fell asleep there.

He understood a new day was starting with the sunlight on his eyelids. He could be easily spotted there; he had to get to town, and get lost in the crowd. He was very hungry, but he had rested a bit by sleeping. He continued to walk, trying not to be seen by anyone. At midday he had reached a small town. People could be seen in the streets here and there. A huge black slave was walking with the heavy things he was carrying. His body shining with sweat was bent double.

Wandering around hungry and thirsty in fear he shuddered all of a sudden. He had seen the Israelite that was fighting with Fetun the day before, his face was wrapped up in bandages. But this time he was fighting another Copt. He had noticed Moses, he shouted excitedly:

"Moses, help me!"

He was expecting him to knock out his Copt enemy with a single punch and save him. However, the remorse Moses felt after Fetun fell flat on the ground and didn't move, and the promise he made to his Lord was fresh in his mind. On top of that, the possibility of being caught and executed wasn't over yet. He asked in a harsh manner:

"Do you fight every day?"

Samiri repeated his request for help:

"Moses, please help me!"

The Israelites were too weak to make a collective move against the Pharaoh. Fighting with Copts one by one wasn't going to ease the pressure on them.

"These fights will only increase the hatred between us", he said.

Samiri didn't answer. He was underneath his enemy once again. Moses screamed in sorrow:

"You are a ferocious man."

And then he said to the Copt:

"Let him go, get out of here!"

The man hadn't taken any notice. Despite the promise he had given to his Lord his anger towards the Copt was growing. In his anger towards him, his desire for revenge from the Pharaoh and his men, the pain he felt from the tortures done to his nation, and the reaction against tyranny that had built up in his soul played the major role.

All of a sudden he remembered his father, mother and siblings. He heard the screams of Ezekiel's sinless wife, and his tiny Abigail who charred in flames. His eyes opened wide, his muscles tightened. He wasn't feeling hunger or fatigue. Suddenly he dived like an eagle, grabbed the Copt by his waist and hurled him a few meters away. He hadn't cooled down yet. Clenching his fists, he advanced towards him. The Copt turned pale. He was shaking in fear on the ground where he had fallen, and was trying to get up. When he saw Moses coming at him he screamed at the top of his voice:

"Are you going to kill me like Fetun?"

The young Prince was astonished. What had happened the day before must have been heard of everywhere. When he returned to Goshen the previous night, Samiri had obviously told with pleasure that he had killed one of the Pharaoh's men with a single punch. He understood that it had been taken as a victory that relieved them from all the injustice that went on for years. This killing he hadn't intended had been whispered from ear to ear with great enthusiasm. When Moses paused the Copt found his tongue:

"O Moses, you don't want to be a reformist, you want to be a tyrant."

These words had increased the astonishment of Moses. How did this man know that he had preferred the way of the righteous, the way of reform, instead of tyranny and oppression? Now, in his face, he was reminding him that he was about to do something against his belief, accusing him of emulating tyranny. He was accusing him of provoking killing instead of settling, evil instead of good. So, everybody had heard his lessons in Goshen. When Moses recovered from his thoughts the Copt was long gone. Samiri wasn't around either. When he looked around he saw sleepy faces sticking out of the windows of the shops made of limestone.

The sun was high, and the heat had become nauseating. He felt his hunger and fatigue in every cell of his body. Where to and how could he escape? The guards would definitely catch him. He thought how useless it would be to run away. He thought it would be better to surrender himself. But if he was to be caught they would have no mercy for him, there was no use in dying for nothing. He drank water from a shop to his heart's content, and thanked his Lord for His treat. Without knowing where he was going, he started to walk out of the town.

He was full of rejection against the tyranny of the Pharaoh and his followers. For this reason he had got excited when he saw the fight and tried to stop it the day before, but he had grieved for the man dying accidentally, and felt remorse. When he saw the fight the following day he had got angry enough to repeat what he had regretted. He was glad the man ran away, he could have done the same thing again. Suddenly, he was startled by a familiar voice:

"Hey, Moses!"

When he turned his head in the direction from where the voice came he recognized Sinuha running towards him. His eyes had filled with tears:

"Sinuha, my dear friend!" he shouted.

They hugged each other. The young deputy minister had dressed like one of the public. He too was in a sweat. Suddenly he took Moses by his arm, he held his steel muscles firmly with his fingers,

"Hurry, you don't have time to waste."

Using what was left of their strength they started to run out of the town. Fire was blazing from their bodies, the boiling sand was wrecking their feet. They ran until they came to a field skirted with a fence. They lay in the shade of the first tree they saw. Sinuha started to speak, panting for breath:

"Soldiers" he said. "They found Fetun's body yesterday. They said that the killer was an Israelite. When you didn't return to the palace, you became a suspect too. Everywhere was searched thoroughly with the Pharaoh's order, but there was no trace of you. Haman had learned about your activities in Goshen through his spies. Supporting his speech with evidence, he claimed that you could have committed the homicide, he said it could be expected from you.

The Pharaoh said 'I want real evidence.' Haman didn't have any witnesses, nobody had seen it happen. There was no evidence indicating that you murdered him. Upon this Haman had to stop talking. Everybody went their own way when the Pharaoh ordered you to be found."

In a sarcastic manner, Moses said:

"My step father must be merciful."

"Moses, stop being sarcastic, your condition isn't that bright. Haman said 'When Moses is caught the mystery will be solved.' The spies that returned to the palace at sunrise said that you had killed Fetun."

"Who did they hear that from?"

"Your bravery was talked about in every house in Goshen last night. Queen Mother said 'Moses couldn't have killed him', trying to defend you. And I said some slanderer made it up to alienate Glorious Ramesses and Moses. Haman looked at me in a hostile manner. The Pharaoh was confused, he didn't know who to believe. At that moment they said that an informer had come to the palace. We were all ears. It was the son of Atoni, a leather merchant. He said that you were wandering around in the town wretched, and that you wanted to kill a free citizen of Egypt in order to defend a slave named Samiri, and then added: 'He is the murderer of Fetun.'"

Sinuha's Nile blue eyes met the brave looks of Moses. He had understood that Moses had killed Fetun.

With a sad voice, Moses said:

"I hadn't thought of killing him, it was totally an accident."

"I believe you my friend, however the Pharaoh and his men have agreed that you murdered him. And you know what a free Egyptian being assaulted, let alone being murdered for a slave means in the palace."

Moses slightly nodded his head as if to say "yes." The calmness in his eyes had given way to worry. A half-naked shepherd passed a little ahead of them with his small herd of a few cattle. He was so busy with his animals he didn't even look in the direction they were in. As Sinuha stood up from where they had hidden not to be seen by the shepherd he said:

"I know that you wouldn't kill anyone on purpose. They detected real danger signs in this act of yours. Because this is actually a rebellion, a resistance. It is an effort to back up the Israelites that have suffered. If it had been a regular murder, the palace wouldn't have made so much of it."

. ".."

"The Pharaoh is ready to sacrifice you, he had a regiment of Amun guards sent to town. I left the palace without anyone noticing. I begged to the God of Joseph to find you before the guards."

After catching his breath he smiled and said:

"Without the help of the God of Joseph, I don't think I could have found you so easily."

Moses smiled, but with the concern of being caught, and his hands and feet being cut off diagonally and then being killed, he was looking around. Sinuha hugged him affectionately:

"My dear brother, you have to go away. You should go east, and cross to Sinai from the north of the Red Sea. You will only be safe there."

Sinuha held out the bag full of food he brought with him and his waterskin to Moses. He also gave the white cloth on his head and his sturdy sandals to him. Two lines of tears ran from his blue eyes. Moses' eyes were wet too.

"Godspeed my friend, I swear upon the God of Joseph we will meet again."

"Thank you Sinuha, do pray for me."

"May God help you!"

After being sure there was nobody around, Sinuha quickly disappeared. Moses put the waterskin on his back and hung the bag on his shoulder. He put on the sandals Sinuha gave to him and wrapped his head with the cloth. He walked away, out of Memphis, with quick steps.

He walked a fair distance with fast steps. There wasn't a single shack or a field around him; he was all alone against the tyrant Pharaoh. He didn't have any other choice but to trust Allah and take refuge in His guidance. He stopped for a while, and took a deep breath. Then he opened his hands to the sky and prayed:

"O my Lord, save me from these tyrants!"

He walked without stopping at all until it was dark. Finally he had reached an oasis, there were palm trees around him. He sat leaning on one of the trees, he fell asleep straight away.

* * *

He woke at dawn, took out the food in his bag and ate some. There was nobody around. Thinking he should get going immediately he started walking. After walking for a while he had reached an endless sea of sand. The desert was so hot that Moses was melting as he was making way, the sun was pouring flames on him. He drank a few sips of water from his waterskin. Bones of animals could be seen in the sand. A yellowish desert lizard looked at him with timid eyes and then disappeared. He looked towards the horizon, nothing but desert plants that were used to life without water could be seen. How was he going to find the way to the Red Sea?

"O Allah! I believe you will send me in the right direction" he shouted. He was going towards Sinai with difficulty. It was a long journey. He didn't have enough food or water with him. Upon Sinuha's warning he had set off immediately into the endless desert without sufficient provisions or a guide. A flock of vultures flying high had been following him for hours, he could hear them shrieking frequently.

His only hope was his Lord. He had totally submitted to Him, taken refuge in His guidance. The Pharaoh was after him to do what he hadn't done when he was a baby, to torture him to death. Soldiers were looking for him everywhere. However he totally believed that the Divine Power that took him under its wings since he was a baby would protect him now too, and that it wouldn't let his enemies capture him.

He Was Being Tried among the Waves of Life

S ometimes alone and sometimes joining caravans he came across, he finally reached the north of the Red Sea. When the day before he was walking on sand dunes, now thin green grass had started to appear around him, and a crowded flock of birds had appeared in the sky. As the sun was sinking into the ground like a red tray, he came across a small creek. An acacia tree by the creek had colored its branches red and spread its beauty into the sky generously. He jumped into the creek joyfully and washed himself. He drank the crystalline water to his heart's content and then lay under the acacia.

At the break of dawn he left this oasis too, he had plunged into the sand dunes again. He was opening his waterskin with prayers, and only drinking a few sips of that holy water. The white cloth Sinuha had given him to protect him from the sun was on his head.

He kept on walking with great difficulties. Sometimes endless sand dunes, sometimes rocky hills, and sometimes a village under palm trees could be seen. And sometimes he would see wooden cogwheels on water wells squeaking musical sounds and be happy. Then he would smile and run towards it with great joy, say "in the Name of Allah" and fill his waterskin. The provisions in his bag had finished already, but he wasn't hungry, he would go to sleep hungry and wake up with a full stomach. Sometimes a villager would offer him two dates and that would be enough for him for a whole day. He had lost weight, and he was looking shaggy. His sweaty loincloth had stuck to his big boned body. He was trying to walk, head down, barely dragging along the sandals on his feet, drifting around among sand storms. Nothing but the sound of the sand moving under his feet could be heard. There was no longer green grass or creeks to come across.

As the sun was moving towards the west, preparing to say farewell to Sinai, he reached a well. He was going to pass the night there, under the stars. When he lay on the sand he felt the hot wind that licked his body touch him,

"O Allah, not a single living creature can stand this soft sand or the strong wind that sweeps everything away." Sand dunes were continuously changing shape and turning into new dunes with the harsh wind. "I'm not sure that I can find my way, please show me the way", he said.

He was tired, his eyelids grew heavy. Suddenly he was startled by the voice of an old man with a white beard:

"Moses, son, you are close to Midian. Walk patiently in the direction from where the sun will rise, you will be there before sunset. When you see the palm trees proceed to the village behind them."

He woke up. The hot wind of the day had given way to an unbearable frost. He was cold, his thinned body was shaking. He thought that the old man he saw in his dream must have been Prophet Abraham. He sat down, opened his hands to the sky, the stars were shining, he prayed lengthily. Then crying he prostrated, and stayed like that.

With the sky lightening up he started to walk towards the sun. As the saffron yellow light ball rose slowly, his tongue started to feel like a piece of wood in his mouth. After taking a few sips of the boiling water in his waterskin he headed towards one of the sand dunes that were often changing place. Tumbleweeds were winding around his feet. They had died under the flames of the sun, and had become dead weed.

* * *

Moses was using what was left of his power, being patient with the difficult nature. He climbed another rock face. When he reached the top of it he joyfully shouted:

"Thank you Allah!"

The palm trees in his dream were a little further ahead. It was as if they had glided to the middle of the desert with their emerald wings. "This must be Midian" he murmured. Ahead of him was a large well with Bedouin shepherds and a herd of hundreds of sheep around it. Water was being pulled from the well in big waterskins and poured into wide gutters, again made of leather, the animals were drinking from it happily to their hearts content. The cheerful songs of the shepherds were filling the air. He started to run, his feet sinking in the sand. It couldn't be called running, he was actually rolling in that direction.

When he got close he greeted the shepherds. He snuggled in with hundreds of sheep in front of the gutters and drank with them to his heart's content. His hair was all sticky, and his beard looked messy. The shepherds who stopped singing were looking at this exhausted looking stranger with curiosity. Moses raised his head from the water and smiled at them. The water drops trickling from his hair and chin, wetting his whole body, were shining under the scorching sun. Water that gave life to living creatures had helped him recover a bit. Shielding his eyes with his hands he looked for shade. A little further ahead two beautiful girls were standing next to palm trees, trying to prevent their herd going to the water. He was surprised, even though he was tired he didn't sit down, and walked towards them. Softening the tone of his voice:

"What are you waiting for?"

"The shepherds. We can't go while they are there."

"But there are so many of them."

"There's nothing we can do, we shall wait until they are finished."

"Aren't there any men to take care of your herd?"

"Our father is old, and he has nobody but us."

Moses was facing a scene that would disturb anyone who hadn't lost their human side. He turned his eyes to the well. One group of shepherds had gone and others had replaced them. Even though a long time had passed, the number of sheep at the gutters hadn't decreased. From where he was crouching he said:

"Your turn will never come."

"We wait like this every day."

The owners of newly arriving herds were ignoring them and going to the gutters, taking their turn. Whereas they should help these young girls, and allow their herd to drink water. Moses was a foreigner, he was in a place he didn't know at all. He had no support in this desolate oasis. On top of that he was wanted, there was a merciless enemy on his tail. However, all this negativity didn't stop him from doing the right thing. Disregarding his fatigue he stood up, and went to the well.

"Hey shepherds, move back. Allow these girls' herd to drink water" he shouted.

The shepherds looked at each other amazed. How could this foreigner tell them what to do, who did he count on? Who was this man that was obviously exhausted? Even though they were plenty, they held back. People were more impressed by spiritual power and the way one looks. The power that put fear in their hearts was not the body of Moses, but his spirit, the Bedouin shepherds of Midian pulled back their herds from the gutters. When Moses pulled water with leather waterskins and filled the gutters again, the herd of the girls came to the water. As if he hadn't helped at all, he bowed his head and walked towards the shade of the trees.

As the ball of flames in the sky turned towards the west, the animals had started to make way towards the village twisting and turning between the palm trees like a snake. The sound of bells gradually decreased and then couldn't be heard. As the shepherds were done they were leaving the well, looking at him with fear in their eyes. Finally Moses was alone again; hungry, wretched and exhausted. He had only eaten wild fruit for days. When he opened his heart to his Lord, his eyes filled with tears. As his body took refuge in the shade of a tree, his soul and heart took refuge in the shade of Allah.

"O Allah" he cried out. "I'm in a foreign land, I'm lonely, I'm alone, I'm weak, and I'm helpless. I take refuge in your grace. I need every good thing that you will give to me."

This was deep loyalty expressing all the feelings in his heart. As Moses lowered his hands the sun was about to disappear among the palm trees. Suddenly, he was startled by the sound of approaching footsteps. The sound of inlaid sandals brushing against soft grass was coming from the dusty path that stretched to the village. When he turned his head in that direction he saw one of the girls that he had helped water their animals a little while ago approaching with fast steps. He bowed his head and waited. The beautiful girl, who he later learned was named Zipporah, called out in a timid manner when she was close enough for Moses to hear:

"Truehearted stranger, my father is calling you to pay your fee for watering."

Zipporah had come modestly, just as a virtuous girl would do when she came across a man she wasn't familiar with. No showing off, nor effort for seduction could be seen in her moves. When Moses raised his head they caught each other's eyes for an instant. Her face turned red. Along with the shyness in the girl's moves there was also clarity in her speech. She hadn't beaten about the bush, without being indirect, she had said it straight out at once. This turn of phrase was an expression of her clean nature. For mannered girls would naturally be embarrassed when they talked to unfamiliar men, they wouldn't ramble on, or act in a way that would excite others, and choose the most direct expression possible.

The old father's invitation was an answer from the sky to the prayers of Moses who was wretched, an instant reward for the favor he had done to the girls. However, because Moses had never expected rewards for favors he did, he felt offended by this offer. But at the moment he was lonely and hungry, therefore he had no other option but to accept this offer.

"Let's go" he replied.

Zipporah walked ahead of him to show the way. Moses was following her a few steps behind; with his head down he was proceeding thoughtful and sad. They walked along a narrow trail that twisted and turned, decorated by various fruit trees and colorful flowers. Houses encircled by wooden fences could be seen around, dogs' barking and sheep bleating could be heard, herds returning from the meadows were peacefully entering their barn, the scent of cow dung and hay were mixing with the smell of flowers, gardens were gradually turning gray.

The young girl stopped when she came to a garden encircled by a fence. She calmly said:

"This is our house."

An old man with a white beard welcomed them at the door, and with a voice coming from his heart he said:

"Come in, welcome."

Moses remembered that wonderful night on the shore of the Red Sea. This house was very similar to Ezekiel's modest house. They had just passed the porch when he found himself at a beautiful meal. Fresh meat just taken of skewers, round meatballs, various meals made of fresh vegetables had been put in front of him. With a sweet smile the old man said:

"Eat, my son, don't be shy, fill up your stomach. We treat all our guests this way, it is a custom of our forefathers."

When he saw Moses being shy,

"Don't think of it as being in return for your kindness."

Now it was time for fruit. The old man started to talk again:

"This area is called Midian. It is a very green area we inherited from our forefathers. Tell us, who are you, where are you coming from and where are you going to?"

The old man was very trustworthy in all aspects. Moses told him all he had been through, without leaving any of it out, and all in order. He mentioned the tyranny of the Pharaoh and his followers, the self-sacrifice of Ezekiel and Asiya. He told everything from the murder he committed in Memphis to Sinuha's bravery.

The old man and his daughters were listening to him quietly. When he finished and bowed his head, the old man started talking:

"Misfortunes of the innocent are trials to raise their spiritual levels and make them closer to Allah. If one welcomes problems he encounters with patience, he can reach very high levels. Allah tests those He loves by giving them troubles sometimes, humans reach holy amnesty through trouble."

He continued to talk smiling:

"They call me Jethro. Don't worry, you're safe here. Midian is within the Amurru Kingdom."

Moses' need for trust was more than his need for food. Jethro saying "don't worry" had made him feel safe. He was glad that Midian wasn't ruled by the Pharaoh. He murmured "his tyranny hasn't reached here."

Jethro understood from the change on his face that his heart was relieved too. For an instant he thought about his children. He was aware that the fields weren't appropriate for them. He was sad, but he couldn't find trustworthy and strong men for them. In the trembling light of the torch first he looked at Moses, and then at his daughters. They looked even thinner than ever to him.

Prophet Jethro was sent by Allah as a Prophet to the People of the Wood. He invited his people to the unity of Allah, however they hadn't taken his advice. The People of the Wood had abandoned him, left him alone with his daughters in Midian. But he wasn't cursing his people, he was still trying everything for their guidance to truth.

Zipporah's compassionate looks locked on her father. Both she and her sister were having difficulties working in the field, grazing their herd, and squabbling with disbelieving shepherds at the well. Their bodies were crushed under heavy weights every day. They desired to protect their honor in accordance with Allah's orders, be the woman of their house, and mother of their children. She believed every truehearted woman with a sound nature would be annoyed by working with vulgar men. She looked at Moses out of the corner of her eyes. This noble young man had already proved his courage and true-heartedness with what he had done at the well, even though he was a stranger, he had fearlessly advanced on the shepherds and managed to send them away from the well. Whereas however strong a stranger is he is still weak.

Speaking with his head down and the virtue in his looks indicated he was a trustworthy person. She was thinking that Moses was the person she was looking for. This young man could be the one that could save them from squabbling with shepherds and the burden of farming. Her feelings were clear, she told her thought without beating about the bush:

"Father, you can hire this stranger as a shepherd, I believe it will be good for us."

His daughter's idea had relieved Prophet Jethro. Zipporah who had felt her father's happiness added this sentence to her words:

"This stranger is very strong and honest."

After looking over Moses, the Prophet asked,

"How do you know?"

When the young girl recounted what had happened at the well Prophet Jethro was even happier. He looked at Moses fondly. He was listening to the conversation quietly with a sweet smile on his face. He thought they were a good match for each other. He noticed the natural sparkle in his daughter's eyes that wished to marry a brave and honest man. He had seen the same sparkle in the eyes of Moses too. Power and virtue in a man would always attract a truehearted young girl, that is what his experience was whispering to him. Turning to Moses,

"Son, you must be patient with the trials of life. I want to make you an offer."

After taking a deep breath,

"I want you to manage my farm. If you accept my conditions, all I own in Midian will be yours."

Moses was all ears.

"Will you marry my daughter Zipporah?"

The face of the young Prince turned red. He bowed his head. He was happy, but he was expecting a different offer. This unexpected question had surprised him.

"My second condition is that you stay here for eight years and work with us. If you make this period ten years it will be your grant to us. We will never cause any difficulties for you while you are with us."

Moses fell into a deep silence. He had been raised spoon-fed in the palace, and educated in colleges and the academy. He had been chased and pushed into loneliness and hunger after the weird murder he had committed under the influence of the hatred in him against the Pharaoh and his regime. He had drifted away from the land he was born, into a foreign land. Divine Power was now pushing him to shepherding. "How weird, from being a prince to being a shepherd", he murmured. For sure the palace had a unique ambiance, customs and a special atmosphere that influenced the human soul. Whereas, on farms there was a very different life style.

Everybody had gone quiet, they had bowed their heads, waiting for his decision. He looked at Zipporah, she was beautiful and attractive. Even if poor people are beautiful, and their hearts are full of goodness their looks prevent them from gaining place in the hearts of the rich. However Moses decided that this offer was a part of his trial. After a short silence,

"I accept your conditions" he answered.

Prophet Jethro smiled and asked,

"Eight or ten years?"

Eight years was a fairly long time. Was he ready to give up the comfort he was used to for that long? Was his sensitive soul going to endure eight years of hardship?

"I accept eight years for now. I would like to decide on continuing to ten in the years ahead."

"Can we take your word?"

"I will keep my promise all the way."

Therefore, he decided to appreciate the blessings given to him by Allah after a short period of fear of being caught, hunger and hardship. Allah who had tried him with the wild waves of the Nile when he was a tiny baby was now trying him among the waves of life.

The Bushes of Roses
Smell Roses Too

a large lounge with gold gilded curtains. The floor covered with bluish white colored Sinai marble. Vases filled with flowers in the window sills and on the engraved tables in the middle. A stern, handsome man with a wide forehead on a throne studded with precious stones in the background. The sun which was hiding behind clouds and then peeking out, was hitting the colorful glass in the window, turning the marble the young king was dreaming on into a rainbow.

A guard with muscles of steel moved towards the middle of the lounge with fast steps, bowed respectfully in front of the king and said,

"Chief Commander Niyere wishes to be accepted."

"Send him in."

A little later a soldier with brave looks entered the lounge among his four well-built assistants. The glimmer in his eyes showed his joy of his success. With a self-confident manner,

"We brought them all your majesty."

"Was their chief caught?"

"He is a priest your majesty, he is outside."

"I want to see him."

When the Chief Commander made a gesture for him to be brought in, an ugly man with a shaved head was brought into the lounge between two guards. When the young King saw this hairless man whose head was shining in the sun he stood up in amazement,

"So it's you Priest Adonis."

The priest was amazed too.

"Prince Sepi" he murmured.

With a harsher voice the king said:

"Not Prince Sepi, Amurru King Great Sepi."

"I mean, Glorious King."

"Tell me you Memphis fox, what were you doing in that deserted temple?"

Adonis had pulled himself together quickly, impudently he said,

"A mission, Glorious King."

Keeping up appearances, with a sarcastic manner King Sepi said:

"Isn't your place by your vile vizier?"

Turning to Chief Commander Niyere:

"Who else was there in the temple?"

"A few officers, a lot of soldiers, one priest and three beautiful girls."

"Tell me Adonis, why do you have so many soldiers in a deserted temple within our borders? Whereas a few miles away you have hundreds of warriors."

"It's Haman's order your majesty."

"There is definitely evil wherever you are."

".."

"Ten years ago you prevented me attending the welcoming ceremony for the Pharaoh. You had said that my mother had an accident, that I should return to Megiddo immediately, and sent me to my country. However you had lied, there wasn't such an accident. You didn't want me to be with Moses and Sinuha. Tell me, why did you do so?"

".."

"Talk you scum, do you want to die?"

"Haman had given orders."

"His time will come too."

"Noble King, the Amurrus were in a friendly relationship with Egypt for years, however now it is said that you are getting on well with the Hittites."

"My father Kuha didn't know Egypt enough. He thought he was friends with you, but he died a few months ago. However, friendships between countries are based on self-interest. I know well that Egypt's friendship is only for its own good."

The King looked at Adonis disgustingly, as if looking at an insect,

"Do your slaves die from hunger in Sinai? Are the babies of the Israelites still killed? Does Egypt, the center of so called justice, fake justice, still worship the Pharaoh?"

"Aren't you a little too confident?"

"Do you still salute his statues with magnificent ceremonies? Do you still treat a black bull as a god? Poor empire, poor people."

With a threatening expression Priest Adonis said:

"Aren't you afraid of the revenge of Ramesses?"

"The Hittite King Muwatalli is counting the days to invade the rich land of Egypt with his army of tens of thousands of infantry and horsemen, and hundreds of chariots."

Adonis bowed his head.

"I know that Sinuha is the treasurer, but I have been receiving contradictory information about Moses for a long time. What is the truth?"

"Honorable King. Moses is not the son of the Pharaoh but an Israelite waiting for a chance to rebel against his country. There are serious clues indicating that he is in preparation of a revolt against the Pharaoh in cooperation with them. Furthermore, he killed someone of the palace and went missing. Even though he has been sought for ten years, there is no trace of him. We thought he had taken refuge in your country."

King Sepi repeated his question when the priest finished giving his answer:

"Priests, oracles and magicians live in temples. Whereas your temple within our borders is full of soldiers. What is the reason for this?"

"Pharaoh Ramesses, the representative of Amun, the god of the skies and the ground, on earth will not leave this act of yours unpunished."

"Take him away Niyere. Throw him in the deepest dungeons of Megiddo, let the mice gnaw on his flesh."

"As you wish Great Sepi, Great King of Amurru."

Two of his assistants took the priest away upon Niyere's sign.

"Niyere, what else did you learn about the temple?"

"One of the girls in custody insists that she is not a nun and that she was imprisoned in the temple."

"Who is she?"

"She says that she can only tell the king."

"Very interesting, bring that girl to me."

All eyes were on the door. A little later a beautiful girl in a pink dress decorated with shiny scales came into the lounge. She looked very innocent in colorful fabrics stretching to her heels. Despite her beauty and elegance, the trace of people who had suffered could be seen in her eyes.

"Come closer angel faced beauty. You said that you aren't a nun even though you were staying in the Amun temple. You look noble, tell me, who are you?"

The fairy girl wrapped in pink tulle walked towards the throne without taking her green eyes off the Sinai marble on the floor. When she came exactly in front of the king, she bowed respectfully. And then she burst into tears all of a sudden. Everyone was surprised but most of all King Sepi. After wiping her tears with her delicate fingers she started talking as if begging:

"Save me Noble King."

After stopping momentarily,

"Excuse my insolence my King, I have been disrespectful by crying in your presence, I lost myself for a moment."

Trying to hide his amazement Sepi asked:

"Who do you want me to save you from?"

"My father."

"..."

"Your majesty, there are people that seem to have been created for evil, they enjoy poisoning at every chance, just like a snake."

"You are talking like a riddle."

"I'm Tiye, the daughter of Haman. I have been a prisoner in this deserted temple for ten years. You aren't going to deliver me to my father, are you?"

King Sepi turned pale, his face looked like it had been mummified. Trying to hide his amazement:

"Sinuha, my true friend" he murmured.

Two lines of tears ran from his eyes. Tiye had thrown herself at his feet.

"No Tiye, please" he managed to say quietly.

"So, you are the girl that Sinuha loved madly" he added. "He would read very lyrical and very romantic poems for you. But what a pity you are still separated. Haman really is a very vile man."

Tiye began to speak with an emotional voice:

"It was the day Sinuha was going to return from Memphis, that is one day before the celebrations for the Pharaoh's Nubia Victory. My father had me and my maids taken away from Thebes. Escorted by Ptah guards, we were taken first to the academy in Memphis, and then to the mountain temple where you found us. Priest Adonis was responsible for us. You can't imagine how obdurate and sly he is my Noble King."

Sepi shook his head bitterly,

"I do know Tiye, I know that vile man very well."

"My crime was loving Sinuha, I was treated like a slave for years because I didn't marry Ubiante."

After taking a deep breath:

"Neither my mother nor Sinuha knew about my captivity. The soldiers of the garrison close to us could be seen from the small window of my room in the temple. But I couldn't notify anyone. I begged Adonis, I said that no harm would be done to him if he let me escape, I offered him a fortune. But he already had more than that from my father."

She stopped, her eyes red from crying were looking somewhere unknown. Murmuring quietly:

"You aren't going to send me back, are you your majesty?" she said.

"What are you talking about Tiye? From this day on you are the most precious guest of my palace. I will definitely let my friend Sinuha know that you are with me and safe."

Tiye's eyes were shining:

"I am grateful your majesty."

"Are your maids here too?"

"Yes King."

"Niyere, bring them too."

Two brunette girls entered the lounge with timid steps.

"Don't be afraid, you are my guests."

The girls saluted King Sepi by bowing as far as they could.

With a voice full of anxiety Maid Tesi said:

"I beg you King, help my princess."

"The bushes of roses smell roses too. You too are no longer slaves, you are honorable and free people. So, as the fairies of Pi Ramesses were wearing silk and using nauseating fragrances every day, swaying in gold gilded lounges, you were suffering in the Amun Temple."

"..."

"Niyere, make our guests comfortable."

After the Chief Commander took Princess Tiye and her maids out of the lounge he asked,

"Do you have any other orders my King?"

"Niyere, we were wishing to find out what was going on in that mountain temple which was interesting Egyptian soldiers a lot lately, but we came across a surprise. However, from now on our country is under a greater threat. Ensure border security. I will not repeat how vile Haman is. And discuss this matter with the representative of the Hittite king immediately.

You Should Have Hope
That He Will Believe

Ten years had gone by, Moses had kept his promise, and extended his stay for two more years at the end of eight years. He had two sons from his happy marriage with Zipporah, one was nine and the other was five years old. His father in law, Jethro, had treated him with the politeness that could be expected from a Prophet, hadn't offended him or given him tasks that he couldn't handle, he had shown all kinds of examples of high morality. However, Moses' last year in Midian had been very troublesome. He was having dreams very often. In his dreams, sometimes he would ride a horse towards the Red Sea with Sinuha, and sometimes he would wander in the gardens of Karnak with Asiya. He had missed Sinuha. His words "My dear friend, you must go to the east. You will only be safe there" were still fresh in his mind. Had Sinuha rejoined his Tiye?

He had thought about his family a lot this last year, he wondered who was still alive? A voice within him whispered that they had returned to Egypt. His sister Miriam and his brother Aaron that he had never seen were in his dreams.

He had been living in the dark since he settled in Midian. He hadn't got the slightest information from his country for years. He missed his country, he was homesick. His feelings were telling him that the danger had passed, that the Pharaoh had forgotten him. He thought he was busy building his fortune. He had shared his thought of returning to Egypt with his wife. His wife who was pregnant had said "It's up to you, but if you wish we could go after our child is born." This thought had seemed reasonable to Moses at first, but he couldn't get over his home sickness. He said "There's still a long time until you give birth Zipporah, our journey is very short, if you wish we can go now." Zipporah was ready to go with him. His father in law had left it up to him too. He couldn't understand himself, in this place he had stayed happily for ten years, now he couldn't stand staying one day more. Whereas he had got used to all kind of hardship on the farm, he had taken on the customs and simplicity of the village. Yet, he was feeling that he wasn't controlling his will, Divine Power was steering him towards the country where his nation lived, to struggle again. He was being pushed to walk the difficult journey that he had walked years ago alone, hungry and thirsty, but now with his family. Without doubt he was being steered to new experiences and training in all aspects. To gain features a leader must have, he had to pass through certain experience stages. Because, his nation which he was going to be the savior of, had declined in all aspects, lost its determination and ability to struggle, due to excessive oppression and humiliation. They needed a strong leader with a strong will who could stimulate them.

* * *

It was a windy winter day when they set off. They were going to take the long way, avoiding the desert. For this time he had his wife, children and even a small herd with him. They headed north. Zipporah had mounted the gray horse with her younger son, and Gershom was on the chestnut horse. Moses was proceeding on foot, preventing their small herd from going astray with his long staff. They were trying to pass far from settlements, and stay away from trouble. After passing the Red Sea, the danger was going to increase.

* * *

Days passed by. They had obtained water from a few oases, and got some food, without encountering any difficulties they had made half way. One day, as the sun turned red and inclined to hide, Mount Sinai appeared with all its majesty. It was exactly half way to the Red Sea. They were aiming at reaching the forest on the skirts of the mountain before dark fell. It must be safer there. But, as it got dark the cold and wind increased, the children were cold. The horses were listening into the distance every now and then, stretching their heads out and neighing strongly, their manes were flying gently towards the Red Sea in the wind. Moses was going to look for flint and try to light a fire.

A pitch black night started. The storm was getting harsher, it was getting even more difficult to find the way. They had dismounted their horses not to lose each other. Moses remembered that terrible night when Sinuha and he had got lost, and passed the night in Ezekiel's house. That wonderful night that had turned his life around.

The herd had totally scattered from the severity of the storm. The horses were standing close covering each other with their manes, there nostrils were dilated. Moses picked up his younger son, and took Gershom by his hand. He had given his staff to Zipporah, they started to proceed towards the skirts of the mountain, walking slowly. They were chilled to the bone, Gershom and his brother were shivering under thick covers. They had nothing but three horses they had tied to each other left with them.

A little later Zipporah said that she had pain and that she couldn't walk any further. They could hardly hear each other because of the roaring wind. His wife whose labor had started early was writhing in pain. They stopped. They were lost on the skirts of the mountain. They could tell they were among trees from the lightning that was striking every now and then. Moses tied the horses to a tree, and laid down a cover on the ground. Meanwhile, he had seen a very bright fire quite far away. He murmured "This is a forest fire." Lightning that struck a tree could make a strong light like that. Or was it a big fire lit by Bedouins for those who had lost their way? He could find a place to stay, or people to show them the way there.

"Zipporah, I can see a light ahead. Maybe I could find a fire there. You stay put," he said and added:

"Don't worry, Allah is with us."

Moses started to walk towards the valley where he had seen the light. As the wind got stronger he was leaning on his staff, getting closer to the fire quickly. As he proceeded in the valley, he saw that the brightness was spreading from one of the trees. Suddenly something wonderful happened. Dark gave way to light, it was white everywhere, and the whole valley had filled with light spurting out of the tree. Blinded by the light, Moses was trying to shade his eyes with his hands. Suddenly, a sound like thunder was heard from among this holy whiteness:

"O Moses! I am Allah, the Lord of the universe. And without doubt I am your Lord."

Moses had felt this call that took over the sky and the earth with his whole body. He was amazed, shocked, he didn't know what to do, or how to respond. His spirit was floating in a great emptiness, as if he was rolling from mountains to plains, from highlands to the sea. Even though he was created as a human, he was given cognition able to accept and comprehend orders coming from that infinite enlightenment source, he had been raised to the highest possible degree a human could reach. This was the meeting of particle and infinity. Could it ever be possible without Allah's grace?

Moses had understood the fire he saw wasn't for heating purposes. It wasn't fire that he saw, it was a piece of Allah's light, a tiny particle of His brightness.[3]

Yes, this was a miracle.

The extraordinary call continued:

"Moses! You are in the Holy Valley of Tuwa, in our presence, take off your shoes."

This valley where the Mightiest of the Mighty Allah appeared with His flawless attributes was made clean and abundant from that moment on.

Moses was trembling, his whole body was shaking. He had come across the All-Holy Creator that eyes couldn't see and minds could not grasp. He couldn't possibly define the source of the sound. He couldn't understand how he heard or perceived this voice either. He had been spoken to, and he had heard. He couldn't understand what was happening behind the scenes. This was a state far beyond human understanding and thought. He took off his sandals, took them to the entrance of the valley and returned. Only a little while later, he trembled with another sound:

"I have chosen you, so listen to what is revealed."

---

[3] "His veil is the light (in some narrations, "fire"). If He reveals it, the splendor of His Countenance would burn His all creation" (*Sahih Muslim*, Iman, 293).

What an unreachable degree and great honor it was for him to be chosen by Allah among millions of people that lived on earth. What great grace, what a great gift this was.

"There is no god but Me, worship Me. Offer prayers to glorify Me and to thank Me!"

Offering prayers was being emphasized; because offering prayers was the most perfect way of glorifying and remembering Allah.

Allah had commanded that He had chosen him. He had been chosen respondent to His words, that is from then on he was a Prophet. The Sublime Creator was speaking to humanity in the person of him.

The holy message went on:

"The Day of Judgment will definitely come. Do not allow those who don't contemplate it and chase their desires change your target, otherwise you will perish."

Moses knew that in Egypt deeds were done to please the Pharaoh who was accepted as god, he was the only ruler of the world. In this belief the Pharaoh was a very special god that provided the people with happiness and produces with abundance. Pharaohs believed in life after death too. According to them, the symbol of it was mausoleums. All their belongings that they could use in the hereafter were put in their mausoleums. Even their wives, servants and horses were buried with them. According to this belief, the fate of the people was in the hands of the Pharaoh after their death too. He was immortalized by magical rituals. The Pharaoh would grant the right to build mausoleums to his most loyal men, his viziers and priests for their life after death, granting them immortality too.

Whereas the message of the Day of Judgment sent to Moses was going to rule out the wrong belief of the people of Egypt, and reduce the Pharaoh's honor in the eyes of the public.

Moses remembered the warped belief of the people of the palace, where he had lived for years. The people of Egypt believed that after death their spirits would enter various animal bodies in accordance with their scale, and then would return to human bodies. In this case, for the deceased to return to their body, it had to be mummified and preserved. For this reason mummification had become an important economic sector in the country, and it was also making magicians very active. The Pharaoh who was believed to interfere in life after death was gaining great power due to it.

Thousands of oracles and magicians were working in temples to delay and finally abolish death. Allah was clearly indicating the fallacy of this belief, that there wouldn't be immortality on earth, and that the Day of Judgment would definitely come. After all, the Pharaoh was ruling his people by denying the Day of Judgment with the promise of immortality.

* * *

Moses had been overwhelmed during this holy call, and forgot why he had come there. To listen to the holy commands ordered to him, he had drifted to other worlds. In the world of immersion suddenly he was questioned by the Sublime Creator:

"O Moses! What is in your right hand?"

Moses couldn't answer for a long while. He didn't know where he was, or where his staff was. Then, his whole body shaking:

"My staff. I drive my herd, and shake down leaves with it."

The staff was a present of Prophet Jethro. Moses had driven his herd in Midian with that staff. He had brought here his small herd that he had lost now in the dark with it too.

The sublime call coming from the holy light said,

"Put it down."

As soon as Moses obeyed his Lord's order and put his staff down something amazing happened. This lifeless staff suddenly turned into a very big and scary snake that was attacking all around. Moses' eyes grew in amazement. The Owner of the Universe had just made an inconceivably great miracle with a simple staff that was in his hand. This snake couldn't be the staff he had carried with him for a long time. And it didn't look like anything he had seen before. First it had stretched out to a tree and ate its leaves, and then it hit a rock and broke pieces off it. His heart sunk, he almost fainted out of fear, then he recovered and began to run in the direction he had come from without looking back. He didn't think at all to understand this extraordinary event. This was a wonderful surprise his spirit wasn't ready for.

Moses remembered the fear that had horrified him that he felt when he had killed the Copt in the market place of Memphis. He had felt great remorse in him for that accidental killing. Fear and worry had given way to hope with the help of Sinuha.

The holy call was heard again:

"O Moses, do not be afraid, come back, you are safe."

Fear and hope, these two feelings had never left him alone all his life, together they had ruled his world from the beginning. Another message was heard from the holy call:

"O Moses, do not be afraid, hold your staff. We shall return it to its previous form."

Moses returned, he caught the snake by its tail and picked it up. That huge animal suddenly turned into its previous form, that is a staff. He understood his fear was groundless and smiled. The thing that really surprised him was it happening all of a sudden. Didn't millions of dry vine stems, like his staff, come alive in the period defined by fate? The staff turning into a fast moving big snake was an extraordinary event that ripped the curtain of fog, that is why he was terrified. Miracles of life that couldn't be seen, but came alive and moved on earth every second weren't attracting attention. Because they happened secretly they weren't noticed.

This time the miracle had happened the other way around. A living creature's, a snake's, all elements of life had been taken from it, it had been turned into a stiff dead thing. And wasn't he the same before the miracle of coming to life happened?

The holy cry called out again:

"O Moses, put your hand in your armpit, it will come out white as snow."

Obeying the command Moses put his hand in his armpit, when he brought it out he was facing a new surprise. His hand was shining brightly, giving off rays of light like the sun. Whereas his skin was wheat colored, close to dark. Moses began to shake under the influence of the miracles that had happened one after the other, he didn't know what to do. He was looking at his hand which was enlightening his surroundings like a torch in the pitch dark of the night in amazement.

The Divine Power came to the rescue and told him to calm down:

"Bring together your arms which you opened in fear upon your chest."

His Lord was asking him to place his hands on his heart to soften his excitement. And he did it, so his heartbeat slowed down, his hand returned to normal.

The holy call was heard again:

"O Moses, the change in your staff and your hand giving off light are proof of your Prophethood given to you by your Lord against the Pharaoh and his men. Now go to the Pharaoh, invite him to the true path. Because he has increased his tyranny, gone astray and is raving."

Moses, with the title of Allah's Messenger, was being sent to the world's most tyrannical dictator, the Pharaoh. He was going to clash with both the Pharaoh and his own nation in a gigantic ocean, where loads of complex issues existed. The world was going to witness the biggest show-down between belief and disbelief.

The Israelites had lived as slaves for a long time, and had been constantly belittled. Slavery had changed their characters, blunted their ability to struggle. He was facing a society that had mixed up the truth and lies, and that thought superstitions were the truth.

The events Moses had been through one after the other since his birth indicated that he was being prepared for a particular mission. When he was only a tiny baby he had been through many hardships, when he was powerless and in need of protection he had been settled in his archenemy's palace, and grew up under his supervision. He had been tested with the fear of killing a Copt, and tried by staying away from his homeland. Earning his living by shepherding sheep for Prophet Jethro for years in Midian, getting married and settling there were all rings of preparation for this mission. He had been patient and passed the test successfully.

Now, when the tyrant Pharaoh's oppression of the Israelites became unbearable, he was being brought from Midian, chosen as a Prophet, and commissioned to convey the message to him. Moses mustered up all his courage, and spoke to the whiteness that was shining like silver in front of him:

"O Allah, I killed one of them, I am afraid of being killed."

Moses had said this not to give an excuse and be freed from the mission, but because he was worried about being killed by the Pharaoh and Prophethood being interrupted. Thus he was being accurate and precise as he should. He went on:

"O my Lord! Expand my breast for me and make my affair easy to me."

Moses had grown up in the palace, he knew the Pharaoh well. He was the most powerful but most tyrannical king on earth, the ruler of a powerful army. A dictator who had gone so far in denial that he didn't accept any other deities than himself. He was going to invite the Pharaoh and his nation to believe in a single Allah without any partners, his task was difficult. Aware of the difficulty he was requesting help.

"O Lord, undo the knot in my tongue, (that) they may understand my word," he said.

Suddenly his elder brother who he hadn't seen since he was born came to his mind.

"O Allah, I don't think I will be able to answer them alone, assign Aaron too with me. He speaks clearer than me."

After taking a deep breath:

"Even if accidentally, I did kill one of them, I am worried about their desire for revenge."

Moses was right in his hesitation. Because he was going to stand in front of someone who was claiming to be god, invite him to believe in Allah, and explain the wrongness of his way. The Pharaoh's mentor, devil minded vizier Haman would be opposing him too. He knew he was exuberant, harsh, short tempered; and was hoping that his brother was a calm and patient person. He was asking his Lord to give him a helper for the weight of Prophethood that was put on his shoulders. If he was to be killed, there would be someone to carry on after him.

Among the beams of light his Lord's guarantee was heard:

"O Moses, we gave you what you requested, we will support you with your brother. We will give you such strength that nobody will be able to harm you. For the miracles in your hands no tyrant will be able to touch you. You and those who obey you will surpass."

The Lord of the Worlds explained how he should treat the Pharaoh:

"O Moses, go with your miracles, inform the Pharaoh of our orders and prohibitions. Do not allow his rebellious attitude to make you angry. Talk to him softly. Do not upset him so he can listen to you. You must start your work hoping that he will fear my tormenting and believe in me so that you can get a result. If you don't act with hope in your heart that he will believe, you will not have fulfilled your duty of conveying the message."

* * *

Prophet Moses had lived the happiest minutes of his life during his talk with his Lord in the Valley of Tuwa, and taken on a holy mission. He had to go to Egypt as soon as possible, and start conveying the message.

Aaron Was Made a Prophet

When Allah's Messenger returned he found his wife and children peaceful. Zipporah's pain was gone, and she wasn't cold anymore. Their children had hugged their mother and fallen into deep sleep. With the first light of day he gathered his herd which had scattered. He untied the horses.

They set off for Egypt. He wasn't afraid anymore. His Lord had said that He was with him, what else could he ask for? He dreamed of meeting Aaron throughout the journey. He had been told that he would come across him in the Valley of Sharit, a few days journey from Memphis. Keeping on going to the west, he finally came to an oasis on the evening of a vernal day. There was nobody around. He moved towards the wells he had seen in his dreams. He was so excited that his heartbeat could be heard. As he approached the third well, he saw that a tallish, wheat color skinned man in his forties was waiting there. First he screamed out loud:

"Aaron!"

And then he started to run wildly towards him. The tallish man had opened his arms too and was running towards him. First they hugged each other as two seas met, then they calmed down. They stayed hugging for a while, they were both crying. After Moses left Zipporah and their children with Aaron's children in the oasis, he walked to the palm trees with Aaron.

When Allah informed that He accepted the request of Moses in the Valley of Tuwa, the Prophethood mission was announced to Aaron too, and he was asked to welcome Moses. They sat beneath a palm tree. The merciless tyranny of the Pharaoh was discouraging them. They opened their hands to the sky and asked:

"O Lord, what if the tyrant Pharaoh attacks us without waiting for us to complete conveying the message, what if he tries to kill us without giving us a chance of showing our miracles, what if he insults you with words that aren't fit for your dignity, what shall we do, how shall we act?"

Allah said to these sincere people:

"O Prophets, do not be afraid, I am always with you. I see what will happen, and hear your desires. Say to the Pharaoh: 'We are Prophets sent to you by our Lord. Give up tyrannizing the Israelites. Let us take them to the holy land. Know that felicity in this world and the hereafter is for those who walk in the path that Allah wishes. Those who don't accept Prophets and close their ears to their invitation will taste Divine torment which is definite.'"

But the Pharaoh had announced himself god. He was severely punishing those who didn't accept him as a deity.

Moses and Aaron talked about the orders of their Lord for a while.

Aaron:

"Listen Moses, the Pharaoh has been ruling the country from Memphis in the last few years. But he passes the summer in Pi Ramesses, the Golden City in the Nile Delta."

"Where is he now?"

"Memphis."

Pointing with his finger:

"In the magnificent palace behind these palm trees. His fifty eighth birthday was celebrated with a magnificent ceremony two weeks ago."

"Could we go to the palace tomorrow?"

"Let's go."

He was going to be Aaron's guest. They walked with fast steps towards the shacks on the outskirts of the city. Early in the morning they were going to ask for an appointment from the palace. When they sat on the cool porch of a cute house with its garden full of flowers, Moses asked:

"Are they alive?"

Aaron shook his head in sorrow:

"It's been twenty years since I saw mother and father."

After taking a deep breath he continued:

"I was four or five years old. We had fled from the tyranny of the Pharaoh to the north and taken refuge in the land of the Amurrus. Our father was making a living by shepherding. When I was ten years old I had learned everything about you. A few years later, even though they were afraid, they put me in a caravan going to Egypt, and sent me to Memphis."

"Why?"

"They were worried about you, and yearning for you."

Moses smiled with joy, there were tears in his eyes:

"Did my mother love me?"

"So she did. I was going to go to the Valley of Faiyum and find the person my father mentioned."

"Who were you looking for?"

"Someone named Ezekiel."

Amazed, Moses said:

"O Lord, that old man."

"Did you say something?"

"No, carry on."

"My father had told me he was hiding from the Pharaoh's men using the name Absalom. The dam authorities looked at the records and said that someone by that name had worked there for a short time years ago, but had left without leaving an address."

"What did you do?"

"I was left dumbstruck. My father had told me not to say that I was an Israelite. I said that I was a shepherd from Amurru, and that I had come looking for work. I found work in the garden of a rich Egyptian. But even though I waited a long time the Amurru caravan didn't come back."

"Weird, isn't it?"

"A long time later I heard that secret agents of the Pharaoh had caught spies in the caravan. They put them all in dungeons and impounded their belongings. I needed money in order to return to Amurru. I worked a lot, and I was liked in a short time. Then they sent me to the mansion of a noble, I was to take care of his garden. He wasn't like other Egyptians, he was honest and merciful. I found out that he was the agriculture minister of the country, due to his work he stayed very little in Memphis. He had a blond son at your age, he liked flowers so much that he would walk in the garden in the evenings, and talk to them sweetly. One evening he said to me: 'You look like Moses a lot.'"

"You don't say so?"

"That's exactly what he said. Later I found out that this young man was the cousin of the Pharaoh."

"Sinuha."

"Do you know him?"

"Then?"

"He was smart, bold and hard working. A few years later he became the treasurer. It was said that the treasury was filled up with gold by him."

"Why didn't you return?"

"At that time, the winds of war were blowing between us and the Hittites. The Amurru king had died, and his son who took his place had turned his back on Egypt. When the issue of a girl came up too, war was inevitable."

"What girl?"

"The Pharaoh attacked Amurru with all his power. By the time the Hittites came to help he had ravaged many cities and killed the people. It was said that he reached Kadesh, but he couldn't go any further. The Hittite army was like a wall in front of him. A few days later the bloodiest and most difficult field battle in history started, but it was heard that they couldn't beat each other, everybody went back to their country. The Pharaoh was saying he won, and the Hittites were saying they won, it is still unknown who won that war. Didn't you even hear about this war?"

"No, we heard nothing in Midian."

"That's weird. Years later, when Ramesses and the Hittite King Hattusili made a treaty, I went to our village. But it had been destroyed; people had been killed or they had fled. I searched for them a lot, but I couldn't find their trace. I still don't know if they are alive or not."

There were tears in Aaron's eyes, Moses hugged him with all his strength:

"Your life hasn't been much different to mine."

"One day Sinuha called me and said 'From now on you will settle in the neighborhood of the Israelites, and do research there. You will observe their living conditions and find out what they need. But you are only to report to me about this, do you understand, only to me.' I was both puzzled and frightened. Why was I being sent there? Or had he understood that I was an Israelite?"

Moses murmured:

"Sinuha."

"What did you say?"

"Keep on telling me your life story."

"He wanted me to read the history of Egypt from old papyrus. In a short time I had learned the history of both Egypt and the Israelites. I stayed in the Israelite's neighborhood for more than a year. The old villagers told me that years ago a prince named Moses had stayed there for a while, did some research and prepared reports for the palace. I had guessed that you were that prince."

Moses smiled and said:

"History does repeat itself."

"Minister Sinuha called me to his room one day and told me that I was going to represent the Israelites in the parliament from the following day on."

"Very surprising."

"My dear brother I am still performing this duty. I have done a lot for the happiness of our nation, but nobody knows I am an Israelite. I am guessing the Prince knows this secret. I couldn't ask of course."

"Does he worship the Pharaoh?"

"His room is full of statues, but I haven't seen him worshiping. I think he believes in Allah, but is keeping it a secret."

"Who is the girl that caused the war with the Hittites?"

"Tiye, the daughter of the Grand Vizier."

"Tiye?"

"I heard that she is the girl Sinuha loved. Haman imprisoned her in a temple on the border to keep her away from the prince. But when the Amurru king took hold of the temple he reported the situation to the prince."

"Why?"

"Because the king was Sinuha's friend."

"Who is this king?"

"Sepi. King Sepi."

"O Lord! Sepi and Sinuha."

"You don't know anything, but you know everybody."

"Be patient, I will tell it all."

"When his daughter was captured by the Amurrus, the Grand Vizier stirred up war. However, despite all the searching done by the Egyptian army after the invasion, neither the king nor the princess could be found. Not alive, or even their dead bodies."

"Poor Sinuha."

"The prince went mad when he heard about this situation. Even though he had learned that the girl he loved was alive, he was separated from her again without even rejoining."

"Being tested with trials."

Allah Is the Owner
of All Creatures

*A*aron's duty in the parliament had made it easier to make an appointment, after all, he was considered one of the family. Moses had been raised in the palace of the Pharaoh for years, and had been called the son of the Pharaoh. They were pleased by the Pharaoh accepting to talk with them alone. They passed through the shiny swords of the palace guards and were taken into the throne lounge.

The floor which was laid with blue and green tiles had been decorated all over with colorful flower patterns. The walls were covered with eye catching paintings in which daisies and yellow gentians mixed with each other. Pharaoh Ramesses who was mentioned of as god in all temples was in his throne covered with gold gilding in the middle of the lounge, his arms crossed on his chest with great pride. The symbol of being the Pharaoh, a blue crown was on his head, and a gold necklace around his neck expressed customs. Beneath his waist was covered by a long diagonal pleated skirt, leather sandals kneaded with golden paillettes were shining on his feet. Ramesses' name was remembered with the Kadesh Battle he waged against the Hittites. Pointing his kingdom staff, the symbol of Divine Power, with its end curled like a hook, at the Prophets:

"Come closer" he said.

The two holy people came in front of the throne with the dignity expected from them. The Pharaoh asked with coldness full of arrogance:

"What do you want?"

Aaron started to speak:

"Our invincible Emperor, you know me, and this is my brother Moses. He has something to tell you."

The Pharaoh's looks were locked on Moses, even though he had recognized him there was no change in his attitude. He even turned a deaf ear to Prophet Aaron's "my brother" expression.

He inspected Moses pompously. Without changing the tone of his voice he said:

"What do you have to say?"

Softening the tone of his voice Moses said:

"O Pharaoh, the sky, the earth, and all in it have only one creator, and that is Allah. The Glorious Lord who is the creator of all, and whose life is infinite, sent us to you as a Messenger. Nothing, not even our bodies belong to us, it is only Allah that owns all."

Moses gulped, his throat had dried:

"O Powerful Emperor. We are all guests in this world, surely we will die one day, and return to our Creator. You too are a guest in this temporary world, one day you will pass on from here to another world. While we are living in this world we must sacrifice our existence to our Creator, that is, we should use our body and soul in the way he wishes. Allah will reward our correct actions with significant awards, but if we show denial and disobedience He will punish us."

Moses was speaking with extraordinary modesty, in a convincing manner:

"O Powerful Emperor of Egypt. Everything we see around us, mountains, plains, deserts, seas, the abundant valleys of Faiyum, the Nile that runs thick and fast are all images of our Lord's power reflecting on the world. Birds, insects, butterflies, these palm trees, these beautiful scented roses, these colorful beauties are all colors of that Divine art, its paint. But if the world is seen with heedlessness, these beauties created by Allah will be idolized, called nature, and divided among thousands of gods big and small."

The harshness on the Pharaoh's face was gone, his face had relaxed. He was listening to what Moses was telling curiously, without interfering or getting angry. Moses took heart:

"Allah pledges everyone an immortal, peaceful and happy life after death, promises eternal youth. If we believe in Him, and obey Him, our possessions and reign in this world will stay with us until our death."

Moses didn't want to beat about the bush, and completed his words:

"Allah sent us to convey these matters to you. We are His Messengers, and we are ready to prove it."

Ramesses was looking easier, he had relaxed.

Moses said:

"Glorious King, we have a request for you."

"What is it?"

"Set the Israelites free, let them come with us."

The Pharaoh was acting as if he had just met Moses:

"Congratulations Moses, you spoke very well. Your words are the products of intelligence and logic. It is hard to object to your ideas. However, about believing in Allah and allowing the Israelites to leave the country, I must consult my vizier and priests."

Although Egyptian Pharaohs were the only ruler of the country, the land had expanded so much, and administrative and legal affairs had increased so much that the Pharaoh had transferred some of his authorities to his viziers and high ranking Amun priests. Especially in the last few years Grand Vizier Haman had taken over most of the administration affairs.

Allah's Messengers were quiet, they had conveyed the message.

With a serious and sincere manner the Pharaoh said:

"Now go to the garden, rest there, I will call you."

Upon these words the Prophets left the throne lounge. Guards showed them to the garden decorated with colorful flowers. They sat in wicker seats around the oval pool with colorful fish wandering in it. Young and beautiful concubines that came out of the blue offered them cold and sweet juices from the trays they were carrying. Black slaves started to cool them down with their huge fans. Moses broke the silence:

"Brother Aaron, do you think the Pharaoh believed in Allah?"

"Your words were logical, you expressed your ideas softly. It is certain that he was impressed by your nice words, but I think it is impossible for him to give up his belief."

"Why?"

"The benefit of those around him is a barrier for him to believe."

The heralds dressed in orange that came to them a little later said that they were expected in the green mansion. The two Prophets passed through the granite statues of the Pharaoh and headed towards the Green Mansion that was in a far corner of the garden.

The mansion where special guests were hosted was glamorously beautiful. Bunches of green grapes and bundles of roses had been kneaded on the marble pillars in the lounge. The walls were decorated with mainly green plant patterns. Moses' looks wandered over the gilded curtains that were glimmering, and the yellow green patterned seats. Beautiful smells were coming from the flowers in the small vases on the tables. It was so hot that the guests that filled the lounge had picked the most appropriate spots so they wouldn't be caught by the sun's rays coming through the gaps in the curtain.

The Pharaoh sitting proudly on his gold coated throne had put on his usual pompous attitude. His eyebrows were knitted, and his face had toughened. There was no sign of the softness on his face a short time ago, his face had taken its usual ruthless expression. He had his red crown on which he used on holy days. The whole of Egypt believed in the mysterious power of this red crown, and had expectations from it. His hair that had been dyed black was stretching towards the back of his neck through the side of the crown. Moses remembered that he had told the Pharaoh that his youthfulness would be eternal. He had understood that his hair had been dyed black as a sign of his youthfulness.

Black slaves were trying to cool down their king by waving camel hair fans. Grand Vizier Haman standing on the right of the Pharaoh was looking cold like a statue, he was looking at the Prophets with devilish eyes from beneath the striped cover on his head. The Amun Pontiff Unas was in the lounge too. The loin cloth wrapped around his waist was barely covering his wide hips and his big belly.

The lounge was over crowded with nobles, commanders and high ranking bureaucrats. Even the sullen faces of some district governors could be seen among the crowd. Moses' looks stopped on a pair of blue eyes shining with the light of faith, they greeted each other with their eyes. It was his friend Sinuha.

The Prophets proceeded on the patterned carpet with slow steps towards the throne. Eyes were on them. Moses had noticed the difference in the Pharaoh too. As Aaron had guessed, his opinion had changed after discussing with Haman. He could almost hear the Grand Vizier saying "O Great Ramesses. You are a god, do you want to be a slave? How can you worship another god when the whole of Egypt bows before you?"

The Prophets sat directly across from the throne. Not a single sound could be heard. After gripping his kingdom staff with a hooked end tightly with his left hand, he pointed his right hand at Moses and roared:

"Didn't we raise you since you were a child, didn't you dwell with us for years? You killed one of our friends without mercy, and ran away. Is this what we get in return for our good deeds? You are of the ungrateful."

Wasn't Moses a poor child that grew up by their side? Hadn't they found him in a wooden crate floating on the Nile and brought him into their palace? How could someone who grew up in the palace and was raised by his side until ten years ago now come in front of him with a global argument, claiming Allah is the only creator of the universe? Wasn't he right in despising him and calling him ungrateful?

Hadn't the Pharaoh announced himself a deity? Whereas Moses was inviting him to believe in Allah, and for it to be accepted that he is His Messenger. As if that wasn't enough, he was requesting the Israelites to be sent away with him. How could he dare to make these requests? What did standing in front of him with an idea contrary to his forefathers gods mean? Moses was inviting people to believe in a different deity, trying to cause disturbance in the country.

Moses started to speak in the way his Lord had ordered him:

"You say that you raised me. This situation was a result of the felonious policy you applied to the Israelites. An outcome of killing those innocent babies without mercy. My mother had to leave me to the waters of the Nile to save me from death. I was forced to be raised in your palace under your oppression, instead of in my warm home. Is this what you are trying to reproach me with? What you consider a favor is actually multiple tyranny."

Upon this reasonable answer of Moses the Pharaoh frowned, murmuring started in the crowd.

"I did not kill your friend because of the difference in our belief. That was an unintentional accident. I ran because I was afraid you would unjustly punish me. I believed I would be killed without the chance to prove myself innocent. I came to you to convey Allah's order.

He is the creator of the whole universe and all in it. He is one, His power is infinite. We are His Messengers, our duty is only to announce. Accepting or not, that is a decision you shall make."

The Pharaoh went silent because he didn't think debating would do any good. For this debate could be the beginning of a rebellion against his reign. In a sarcastic manner he asked:

"What does the creator of the universe mean?"

Moses repeated his words he had said in the morning:

"Look at the birds, bees, butterflies and colorful flowers. There is such a perfect stamp on each and every one of them that is particular to only Allah who created all. There is such a stamp on every created thing, that nobody but the single creator has that stamp. Look at the miraculous stamps shining on life, in this world many things are created of one. For example water is a single thing, but with Allah's permission it becomes a source for many things."

Everyone in the lounge was listening carefully,

"In the face of the infinite power of Allah, the Lord of the Worlds, what you are trying to make those who live in the Valley of the Nile accept, isn't even a speck of dust of divinity. If you are one that has reasoning, you will understand that Allah is the owner and possessor of everything that has been created."

With this answer, Moses didn't only blow a hole in the Pharaoh's claim, he also drew the attention of the crowd to the great universe, and invited them to think about the attributes of the possessor of the universe. The thought of believing in Allah, the Lord of the universe, was a big change for those who worshiped the Pharaoh. Because, accepting Allah as a deity meant giving up submitting to orders of other than Him. The Pharaoh was hesitating and worried about the effect of these rather clear and correct words on hearts. He called upon a simple trick that all dictators used. Turning to the people with a sarcastic smile:

"Do you hear these irrational words? What did I ask, and what did he tell? Have you ever heard these words from anyone else?"

The Pharaoh's words weren't heard, for everyone was discussing the words of Moses. Sinuha leaned over and whispered in to his father's ear:

"The Pharaoh has spoken the truth. Before Moses nobody had spoken to him so bravely, or told their belief so freely. Yes, this is the first time."

When it was understood that Moses was going to speak, the discussions in the lounge gave way to silence:

"That Allah is the Lord of you, your forefathers, and all Copts. You are trying to convince your nation that you are their lord, but like everyone else you too are a human that was created by Allah. Like everyone else you too were born from a mother and a father, you grew up eating and drinking, and in the end you will die like every-one else. How can a mortal like you be a god? Your claim of being a deity is an absurd and funny allegation, Allah was the owner of the universe before your forefathers existed."

The discussions in the room had blazed up again. The Grand Vizier whispered in Korah's ear:

"This man must be silenced, he is going to cause dis-union."

Korah answered:

"By denying our gods he is confusing people."

Grand Vizier:

"He should be killed, our economy will be ruined."

The Pharaoh was on the spot. He was only claiming being a deity for the time he lived. However Moses was saying that Allah ruled the past too. This was a very dif-ferent situation.

Turning to his father again, Sinuha said:

"The Copts recognize Ramesses as god, his forefa-thers recognized the previous pharaohs as gods. Where-as Moses appeals to all times. He hit the bull's eye."

Minister Imhotep quietly said:

"This thought rubbishes the official religion of Egypt."

The Pharaoh didn't have an answer for these words, he was aware that it wasn't right to pass it off with silence. Raising his voice he shouted:

"This man who claims to be a Prophet is a lunatic."

With a voice only she could hear, Asiya said:

"Those who are beaten by the truth resort to defamation, slandering or aggression."

Sinuha was upset too:

"The Pharaoh realized debating is no good, so he started attacking, and now he's accusing Moses with lunacy. He is afraid of the religious and political authority turning away from him and being influenced by Moses. He wants to prevent the people turning to Allah."

"You're right son, whereas Moses spoke very convincingly. He explained the power and mightiness of Allah so well."

* * *

The Pharaoh's accusation of lunacy hadn't demotivated Moses. He was determined to convey the message of truth which many tyrant dictators had collapsed in the face of. Even if his opponent was the most barbaric despot in the world who had made his nation his slaves with his unreachable pride, nothing would change. He looked at his brother Aaron. He was standing by him as if to say I'm with you all the way. He looked for Sinuha. He found him delighted. His eyes were saying, I believe you Moses. Gripping his staff tightly, he took a step towards the Pharaoh. Emphasizing the points of sunrise and sunset:

"O Pharaoh, the Lord of the Universe is the Lord of the east, the west, and everything in between. The sun always rises from the east and sets in the west."

Asiya whispered:

"Who could dare to change that? No Pharaoh made such a claim, this one can't either. Has the sun been seen to change these regular movements? It hasn't fallen back or gone forward. This should stimulate even the most heedless minds."

Moses invited them to understand the real purposes behind the scenes:

"These lifeless clouds that hang between the earth and the sky, water our world with their mercy, rescuing all living creatures. Just like a regular army hides when ordered, they sometimes hide, and when they are ordered to their place they come together in an hour or a few minutes and fill the sky, waiting for their commander's order. Of course these unconscious clouds don't know us, they don't run to our rescue themselves, and they don't come about without orders. They act with the order of a powerful and merciful commander.

Grand Vizier Haman turned to the pontiff:

"His every word is dangerous, he is going to distract our nation from our beliefs. This much freedom is too much."

Pontiff:

"If we don't stop him now, we won't be able to stop him at all."

Turning to his father, Sinuha said:

"The enemies of Allah fear nothing as much as the people awakening, and hate nothing as much as they hate those who try to awake them."

Moses was continuing his convincing speech:

"In spring all kinds of vegetables and fruit, hundreds of plants, are all created regularly from something as simple as a seed. All kinds of fruit appear from nothingness and dry soil; raised from dry seeds that are all similar and aren't very different to dry bones. Every spring Allah sends thousands of kinds of food to us perfectly from his generous treasure, complete with scent and taste. Don't all these blessings clearly show us that they are the gift of the Lord who is pitiful, merciful and compassionate?"

Minister Imhotep turned to his son and said:

"Moses is saying very different things. How did he learn them? Very impressive."

"Don't be surprised father, he isn't an ordinary person, he is a Prophet."

Moses carried on:

"The Nile that turns Egypt into heaven, bubbles up from beneath the Moon Mountain in Nubia, for centuries it has run wildly without ending. If the water it gives in six months was to be frozen to ice it would be bigger than Moon Mountain itself. Whereas the source resigned for it in the mountain isn't even one sixth of the Nile. Don't you think about whose power it is that makes this happen?"

Haman's face turned red, he was in dismay. He had lost control:

"Silence him, O Mighty God!"

The Pharaoh turned a deaf ear to the grand vizier's insolence, but he could sense the danger in regard to his future. He stopped the debate and started threatening Moses:

"From now on, if you continue to say that you accept anyone else than me as god, I shall punish you and those who think alike in the most severe manner."

Queen Asiya looked at the Pharaoh full of hatred: "Enemies of Allah use threatening when they can't come up with right proof to put forward" she said to herself.

Actually, most of the people in the lounge were aware that the belief system built by the Pharaoh had many weak points and contradictions.

* * *

The Pharaoh's tyranny was nothing new. He would have the right hand and left foot of those who didn't obey him cut off, and after allowing them suffer for days, he would have them hung on the shore of the Nile. He would have his dissidents tied by their hands and feet to stakes driven into the ground, and leave them to die from hunger and thirst. He had them hung head down in deep wells, and killed with various tortures. He wanted to make Moses submit like them through threatening. This was actually a sign of weakness.

The threatening hadn't discouraged Moses, because he was a Messenger of Allah, he knew that Allah was with him and his brother. Because he was convinced that the time had come to use the miracles his Lord had given to him, he gripped his staff tightly, raised it in the air and said:

"It is understood that you aren't willing to believe in Allah and that we are His Messengers, if I was to show miracles that will prove my claim to be true, will you still not believe?"

Haman turned to Korah and whispered:

"The Pharaoh shouldn't reject this offer."

Korah nodded his head:

"He should show his proof. If he is forced into silence, the idea that we are weak will appear to everyone."

To hide his desperation the Pharaoh smiled in a sarcastic manner:

"If you are insistent in your claim show us what you call a miracle."

Upon these words Moses hurled the staff in his hand towards the throne. That dry stick came alive suddenly and turned into a huge snake, it was twisting and turning flicking out its tongue. The Pharaoh's eyes nearly popped out of his head in fear. He suddenly jumped up and closed his face with his hands. The guests screamed and ran to the walls in fear and confusion. There was great panic in the lounge.

When Moses held the snake from its tail and turned it into its previous form the panic in the lounge calmed down, everybody took their places again. After this miracle, Allah's Messenger put his right hand in his robe and pulled it out. His hand suddenly started to shine like the sun, to give off glaring light in all directions. The miracles that caused confusion among the spectators had scared them, and left their souls in horror.

The miracles had impressed everyone else like the Pharaoh, he had felt his situation getting weaker and weaker. He had to find a solution to save the nobles from these shocking effects immediately. He shouted what came to his mind:

"Moses is a magician."

The Pharaoh looked at the grand vizier as if waiting for support for his claim. Haman had received the sign he was waiting for. He shouted at the top of his voice:

"An awesome magician trying to send us out of our country."

The pontiff joined in on support:

"There is no doubt that it is magic."

Korah couldn't remain quiet:

"He is going to trick us with magic and settle on our possessions."

The Agriculture Minister leaned over to his son:

"Magic is a game of delusion, tricking eyes and feelings. What Moses did was different. They don't really change objects, they transform them into different forms continuously or temporarily. What Moses did was like the work of someone with the power of creation."

"Father, Moses did it with Allah's permission. Do you see the Pharaoh, he is both denying the miracles claiming it is magic, and also turning it into politics, sidetracking."

Support from his closest men had relieved the Pharaoh. He shouted at Moses:

"Are you going to drive us out of our country?"

Moses calmly said:

"Humans are children of soil, as a dead body they will return to soil, their decaying bones will become soil. We have all been created from soil, one day we will return to it, we will account for what we have done. We are showing you miracles so that you will believe in Allah who is immortal, but you are claiming it is magic and refraining from accepting the miracles."

The Pharaoh went silent, he was thinking. The thought of becoming soil had frightened him a lot. Hadn't he had his magicians do magic and cast spells to impress his nation? In that case he could call Moses who turned his staff into a huge dragon, and his hand he put in his robe a light source, a magician. The things that Moses called miracles were similar to what his own magicians did.

Looking at his men the Pharaoh asked:

"What do you have to say?"

Everyone was surprised. What was happening? The man who announced himself a deity and made people prostrate in front of him was now asking for other people's opinions, expecting orders from them. This was the mutual act of all tyrants that felt the ground beneath them shake.

With a voice only she could hear, Asiya said:

"These nobles that wildly exploit the blessings of this country are worried that Egyptians that see the miracles and hear the words of Moses will be subject to him. Even only the Israelites taking place by his side will decrease their influence and shake their dignity. And in the near future it will abolish their economic power. This is what they're worried about."

At that point, Grand Vizier Haman threw his huge body in front of the Pharaoh, prostrated and stayed that way for a while. Then he murmured from where he was:

"O the only representative of gods. My heart wants these Prophets to be killed immediately. However, killing or punishing Moses and his brother will not be in our favor. Our nation will think that we were beaten by him and were desperate."

Haman really believed Moses had done magic. After all, in Egypt religion meant magic and spells. Temples were full of magicians and oracles. After slyly looking at the Prophets:

"There are hundreds of unbeatable magicians and wizards in our country. Let's send out word everywhere, make it heard that we are having a magic contest. We shall promise we will give precious rewards to the winners. Let's compete those who are confident here with Moses. Let's make a fool of them to the whole of Egypt."

After he finished his words the Grand Vizier stood up, bowed all the way to the ground again, and then took his place by the Pharaoh. He looked at Moses and Aaron first, and then at Sinuha, with a bitter smile as if he had won victory.

Sinuha was full of hatred too. He turned to Haman and quietly said:

"Tyrants are seeking simple profits in the acts of believers that invite them to the path of Allah."

Then, turning to his father:

"They think Moses is aiming to take over the country, to have a fortune. They think his noteworthy words and his miracles are all for that cause. Whereas, however profitable, compared to the hereafter, worldly profits are very simple and worthless. Like ordinary glass pieces next to diamonds."

The Pharaoh stood up with great arrogance and pointed his right hands index finger towards Moses. The last rays of the afternoon sun were shining on his diamond ring, blinding the guests. Placing a threatening look on his old face:

"O Moses! We shall gather our magicians and teach you a lesson. Do not worry, you will meet your match."

Moses' face was tensed from anger. He shouted with hate:

"Are you talking against Allah? Are you calling miracles from Allah magic?"

The Pharaoh:

"Did you come to turn us from the religion of our forefathers?"

With a quiet voice Queen Asiya said:

"Their economic profits are based on these silly beliefs of their forefathers, that is why they are holding on to them so tightly. Actually, they don't want to lose their power and fortunes, that is the real reason driving them to denying Allah."

The Pharaoh repeated his last sentence with great rage:

"You will meet your match."

With these words he was challenging Moses. He was going to end the claim of Moses by inviting the most famous magicians and oracles of the country to the capital. Moses harshly said:

"Magicians cannot avoid the curse of Allah."

The Pharaoh wildly laughed out loudly.

"Set the time of the contest yourself."

He was allowing Moses to set the time again to challenge him.

He went on:

"Choose a wide clearance where magicians can easily show their talent, and everyone can easily watch them."

The Pharaoh was confident. While he was laughing, all his golden teeth were seen. In a sarcastic manner:

"Think hard, don't be afraid and change your mind."

Moses kept a straight face. He was happy about the Pharaoh's offer. Being challenged was a good sign. Therefore he was going to be able to convey the message to the Egyptian people too. He whispered some words into Aaron's ear, they agreed:

"The contest shall be held at the Talisman Festival, magicians shall gather in the mid-morning, their talents will be displayed in the wide clearance where military ceremonies are held."

There were still forty days till the Talisman Festival that had been held since the Pharaoh Amenhotep III. Copts would join in this holy day from all over Egypt, the streets of Memphis would fill with hundreds of men and women. Entertainment would go on through the night in the festival that continued for days.

Sinuha smiled:

"Moses made the right choice. If the contest was held earlier not many people would participate, if it was in the afternoon they would scatter from the heat. In the darkness of the evening nothing could be seen clearly, people would be doubtful."

Allah's Messengers walked towards the exit without saying anything.

As Belief Flows Like Floods, the Torment of Tyrants Is Disregarded

*A*s the Talisman Festival approached noticeable activity had started on the river. The surface of the Nile couldn't be seen for the boats. Thousands of people from all over the country were flowing into Memphis on the river, the crowds in the city were growing each day. The festival that year was going to be very different from the others. The famous magicians of the country were rushing here in groups to win the big reward in the contest. Anybody who was confident in their magic could participate in the show, and compete for the reward. Meanwhile Moses had been shown among the master magicians that were going to participate in the contest, the Egyptian people were very excited from days before. The Pharaoh's men were shouting all over the city:

"Come on, come and see the contest of magicians, watch master magicians."

Tyrant rulers amuse people with games and festival ceremonies, therefore they would try to cover the effects of their tyranny on the population. The Pharaoh too was trying to cover up his tyranny by attracting their attention to the contests held every year.

The day of the contest had come, hundreds of Copts, men and women had gathered in the big clearance where military ceremonies were held in Memphis. The Pharaoh's throne had been placed in the most spectacular place of the clearance. A huge bull was brought to the clearance accompanied by ten Amun priests wearing red skirts. Among screams "in the name of our god Pharaoh" the head of the black bull with white spots on its back and rubies shining on its neck was separated from its body with a single slash of a knife.

The bull that had been sacrificed was skinned in a short time, and with its meat being scrambled for, the festival had officially begun. The people were dancing wildly to the music of flutes and harps, drinking Byblos wine from earthenware jugs they brought with them, shouting "god Pharaoh."

A little while later a crowded group of magicians in orange clothes entered the contest area and took their place. They were all shaved, there was no hair at all on their heads. Yasfa, the head of the magicians, bowed with great respect in front of the Pharaoh, and then prostrated. A little while later he raised his head and asked:

"O great god of us, if we beat Moses what will be our reward?"

The Pharaoh's eyes had glowed, smiling devilishly:

"I shall smother you with gold."

The grand vizier and pontiff were in the honor stand next to many ministers, high ranking soldiers, district governors and many nobles. Among the nobles, the Pharaoh's brother Imhotep and his son Sinuha could be seen. Father and son were sitting together again.

Sinuha couldn't stop himself, he leaned towards his father:

"Dear father. If power is not given to Allah in a community, idols will take His place. These fake gods play many tricks to make the people accept them. These magicians are a part of these tricks."

"You're right my son. The magicians are preparing to bless the Pharaoh's power."

"Their talent is subject to the rewards they have pinned their hopes on."

"They have no religious worries, they are doing it all for reputation."

"They are aiming to impress, then they will be rich."

"Don't you see son, they are bargaining upfront."

After being promised money and position he returned to his friends. Meanwhile the famous magician Azur was praising the Pharaoh, screaming he was the only god.

The Prophets splitting the crowd, walking towards the clearing, had excited everyone, all eyes were on them. Moses looked at the magicians with pity. Then he called out to them:

"Shame on you, are you here to invent a lie against Allah? He who invents a lie against his Lord will never escape trouble, you will be destroyed with his torment."

The single sentence of Moses had fallen like lightening in the ranks of those who had diverted to denial, it had discouraged them. Upon these words some of them had decided to withdraw from the contest. Magician Yasfa hissed at those who wanted to withdraw from the contest like a snake:

"Where are you going? Are you afraid of Moses and Aaron? They are eliminating us and playing for leadership. If we lose the contest both our life and our reputation will be in danger, and we will be cursed by the Pharaoh too."

Satur, the magician of the northern districts:

"They want to change our lifestyle and cast us down."

Azur, the magician of the southern districts:

"Whereas we want to live as we wish to, we want to enjoy life in freedom. Let's not allow them to meddle with our lives."

Hathat, the magician of the water snake district:

"Do not fear at all. We shall beat them, and cut the tongues that oppose the Pharaoh. This is war, one side will definitely be crushed, but that will not be us."

Finally the dispute between them ended. Magician Yasfa pointed at Moses and Aaron and called out to the crowd filling the clearance:

"These magicians wish to abolish your gods with their magic."

Sounds of reaction rose from the crowd. Shaking his head Sinuha said:

"Puppets of the system are defending their deviant religion that they don't believe in, for their personal benefit, trying to sustain it even though it is fake."

Minister Imhotep confirmed his son:

"The system is based on making the people slaves to the Pharaoh and his servants. Minds being enlightened with true ideas, hearts filling with strong belief is a big danger for the system. Allowing Moses' religion doesn't suit them."

Prince Sinuha:

"Don't you see Yasfa trying to provoke the people against Moses? But Moses will wipe out these fake gods."

Yasfa devilishly smiled at his friends:

"Don't be afraid, as long as we stay united we will win, do not divide. To divert the attention of Moses and Aaron throw your magical devices all at once. If we beat them we will receive a great reward, if not we will both lose the reward and our reputation" he said to encourage them.

Moses called out to him:

"If I win, will you believe me?"

Smiling sarcastically Yasfa shouted:

"We shall show you such magic and cast such spells that you won't be able to beat us. But if you do, I promise to believe in your Lord."

They were confident in their magic. After catching his friends' eyes one last time, he challenged Allah's Messenger:

"We are ready, who shall start to show their talent first?"

In a careless manner, Moses called out:

"If you are ready, start then."

The Prophet giving them the first turn indicated his confidence. Yasfa's offer hadn't pleased the Pharaoh, he made a sour face. Incomprehensible murmuring rose from the honor stand. With a despising manner Moses shouted at the magicians:

"Come on, throw whatever you will throw."

The hideous scream of Magician Yasfa filled the clearance:

"For god Pharaoh, altogether."

Magician Satur shouted:

"We are followers of the Pharaoh."

Magician Azur repeated:

"We are followers of our forefathers."

The deceived crowd repeated the same sentences like parrots.

"We are followers of the Pharaoh."

"We are followers of our forefathers."

The magicians were so confident that they didn't even wonder if they were going to be successful or not. There was no sign of fear or worry in the eyes of the Prophet either. The magicians threw the staffs and ropes in their hands all at the same time, saying incomprehensible words. A lot of big and small ropes and dry branches turned into horrendous snakes as soon as they hit the hot sand, there were snakes everywhere. Magical devices that had been scattered all of a sudden had taken the shape of hundreds of snakes crawling around.

The Copts were witnessing a magic show that made one's blood run cold. The anxiety that the magic caused in the people was petrifying. Everyone began to run away in fear. Especially women and children were screaming wildly. The magicians had played their game on the people. The Prophets had perceived the ropes and dry branches as dragons too, just like the spectators. Feeling shivering in their souls Moses and Aaron whispered:

"O Allah."

It wasn't actually fear that they felt in their souls, they were worried that the opinion that the magicians were stronger than them would form in the people, therefore their message of belief could lose its effect on them.

Imhotep leaned towards Sinuha and said:

"On one of my trips to Nubia I witnessed something. The magicians there used special staffs with mercury in them and ropes with mercury on them, that expanded with the heat of the sun and started to move to make weird sights. They were influencing the people with such substances that they didn't know about.

Keeping a straight face Sinuha said:

"If they manage to bedazzle the people they have reached their aim."

Moses had shaken off his astonishment, he pulled himself together quickly. Taking refuge in his Lord:

"What you are doing is nothing other than a trick. Whatever you try you can't be successful. However horrendous your magic looks, only those unaware of Allah's power will be scared."

The Pharaoh was pleased. He looked at the nobles in the stands proudly. He waved to his young queen sitting in the gold throne next to him. The beautiful Hittite Princess was keeping up appearances. The people gathered again. They were celebrating the success of the magicians with screams of joy. They were wildly drinking wine from jugs, their half-naked bodies being painted red.

Minister Imhotep was doubtful:

"Is Moses going to be able to win this contest?" he asked.

"Do not worry father. They depend on magical talent whereas Moses depends on Allah. Moses acts with belief, they are after spoils. However rampant the magicians are, they serve a mortal like themselves, Divine Will doesn't rule in accordance with them."

"Your faith is very strong Sinuha."

As hundreds of dragons that spread from the magicians magic continued to radiate fear in the clearance; his Lord reminded Moses that He was with him.

"Do not be afraid, without doubt you are superior, throw your staff right now."

Among the joyful noise of the crowd the strong voice of Moses rang out:

"O magicians, Allah will nullify what you have done. Even if you don't like it, He will prove that he has the true power. The Lord of the Worlds will never allow those who trick with magic and spells in the name of deniers to win."

When Moses, encouraged again by holy guarantee, threw his staff towards the snakes something wonderful that nobody could imagine happened. As soon as the staff touched the ground it turned into a horrendous snake. Among the astonished looks of the people and the magicians, the huge dragon jumped on the magical devices that appeared as snakes with great ambition, and started to swallow them with an appetite. Flutes, harps and shakers all went silent, drunks sobered up. The magicians were dumbfounded in the face of this amazing scene. They had showed all their talent in magic which they were masters of, done all that they could. They were so successful at it that even the Prophets were momentarily doubtful. They were very determined to win, because the great reward was awaiting them. But now they were speechless, they were silent because of their astonishment. Not a single sound could be heard from the Pharaoh or the nobles sitting in the honor stands, they were petrified, they were carried away by what had happened. The staff of Moses was continuing to swallow the images of snakes.

Sinuha's joy was spreading through his whole body in waves. He wanted to shout at the top of his voice: "My dear brother, you are a true Prophet. I believe in Allah and you with my whole heart.", and announce his belief to the whole universe. But it was time to be patient. Leaning towards his father who was watching this amazing event calmly:

"If what Moses has done was magic, after seeing the staff swallowing the snakes, the ropes and staffs would have been seen; that is, everything would return to its previous form. However, there is no rope or staffs around. What they have done is a delusion, Moses' is real."

"I think you're right."

"The magicians' talents were useless, disappearing, just like a dream. See, all of their magic evaporated. The Pharaoh and his followers have been beaten, they have been degraded. Just like a glow fly they burned out after glowing for a short while. Just like Nimrod against Abraham. Denial has to come face to face with the truth to fade away."

When there were no other ropes or staffs wandering around in the shape of a snake, Moses held his dragon from its tail and turned it into its previous form. The clearance had fallen into silence, the Pharaoh's face had turned yellow as if it had been mummified.

Using his intelligence he had ruined the coalition between the Hittites and the Amurrus, he had trampled down Syria from one end to the other with his well-trained Amun troops. He had invaded Phoenician cities one by one, and gone as far as the gates of Byblos. He had caught up with the famous Hittite King Hattusili around Kadesh, and waged an awesome war against him. He had finally stopped the Hittites, and made a peace treaty. He had married Hattusili's daughter Nefertiti, ensuring the treaty to be long termed. He had held Crete, Babylonia, Assyria and Cyprus to ransom. He was the conqueror of Nubia, he had returned from his expeditions with slaves and spoils. But now he was being beaten by someone he raised. How could hundreds of magicians not beat a single man?

The Pharaoh woke from the sleep he was in with the soft voice of Queen Nefertiti:

"Noble Pharaoh. Aren't you afraid of offending, attracting the rage of this God that you don't know at all? He wants to take his nation and go to the desert, let him go."

The Pharaoh smiled unwillingly.

Dead silence took over the clearance. Everyone was waiting for the end of the contest. Suddenly, Yasfa, the leader of the magicians, and then the others said:

"We believe in the god of Moses", and prostrated altogether.

This development caused a new excitement among the Pharaoh and his men who were in great amazement. Ramesses stood up from his throne in anger. His eyes were popping out of his head, and his face turned red:

"What are you saying Yasfa, I misunderstood, didn't I?"

"No my King, you understood right, we mean the Lord of Moses. If what he did was magic he couldn't have beaten us."

The Copts didn't know what to do. They had thought that magicians from all over the country were going to beat Moses, incapacitate him. However the magicians, who had just prostrated in front of the Pharaoh calling his name, were now confessing that they were wrong, accepting Moses was sent by Allah, and prostrating to his Lord.

Sinuha couldn't stop himself:

"Dear father. See, the country's legendary magicians are taking sides with Moses. When he loses the magicians his throne will only depend on military power. No power without a belief can hold up the throne alone. This is the real fear that worries the Pharaoh and his men."

"Yes son, the Pharaoh's throne is being shaken off its foundation. How do you evaluate this sudden change in the magicians' world?"

"Dear father, the magicians know the limits the art of magic has reached very well. Therefore, they understood right away if the miracle of Moses was magic or created by a superior power, they saw they were facing a miracle. Those who are experts in their art subdue to the truth more easily. They saw the truth and gave up uselessly challenging it."

"But tyrants don't understand how holy light enters one's heart, they think they can rule the souls of people too, direct their hearts in the direction of their choice."

As the magicians kept on prostrating some of the priests started to prostrate too, it was spreading. This was driving the Pharaoh crazy. He roared in anger:

"Ungrateful people, you can't believe in their god."

Moses was watching it all quietly, thanking his Lord for not disappointing him. The Pharaoh shouted again:

"Get off the ground you fools, I am your god, beg to me."

There was no movement in those who were prostrating, nobody stood up, their heads were on the ground. As minutes passed new ones were adding to them, they were no longer people who changed direction with orders. The Pharaoh couldn't understand that no power could conquer hearts once they had been enlightened by Allah's light.

"What do you think you are doing, how could you believe in the god of Moses without my permission? Return to your gods, or you will be sorry."

The Pharaoh couldn't comprehend the mystery of the change in his people, he was murmuring "Didn't they gather to reject Moses' invitation."

Queen Asiya looked at the magicians prostrating and said:

"O man with blunt emotion, from now on their hearts cannot even listen to themselves. Do you think they will ask for your permission to put out the light of truth that was born in to their souls?"

Her maid was crying:

"O Compassionate Queen, I want to believe too", she groaned.

"Wait my darling," she whispered.

There wasn't anything the Pharaoh wouldn't do to not lose his reign, he could commit any crime for this. Its protection was based on defending his divinity.

With the magicians changing sides, the Pharaoh had been humiliated in front of his people; the rightfulness of Moses had become apparent. He made another move:

"So, Moses was your mentor, that's why you submitted to him. Or else why would you surrender to him?"

After looking around devilishly:

"You scum, did you make a previous agreement and set a trap for me? It can be seen that you too, like Moses, are traitors trying to ravage the country. Your aim is to make Egypt weak."

The Pharaoh's anger was growing as he saw his words weren't effective; he wasn't even considering that Divine Power could have raised the curtain of denial over eyes. Like wild animals relying on their strength, he bragged about smashing power. He clenched his fists, and clamped his teeth, his face changed color. With a voice like lightning:

"Fools, you will learn what it is to turn away from the Pharaoh, you will pay for it."

Haman had rejoiced:

"The price of believing in Moses must be paid."

The Pharaoh couldn't control his anger:

"Your punishment will be a lesson for the people of Egypt" he shouted.

Haman turned to Korah:

"The Pharaoh is showing his real face."

The Pharaoh roared again:

"Rebelling against your country are you!"

Sinuha was troubled:

"Rebelling against their country, what an excuse!"

The Pharaoh was considering the magicians prostrating, believing in Allah, as rebelling against their country, as treason. Finally, he chose the ugly method that dictators chose when they felt they were in danger:

"I will have your hands and feet cut off on opposite sides, and have you hung on trunks of palm trees."

The Prophets took refuge in Allah against the vile tyranny of the Pharaoh. The voice of Yasfa who was prostrating among the magicians glorifying Allah was heard:

"There is no importance in our hands and feet being cut off and killed, without any doubt we are going to return to Him. We all believe in the Lord who created everything out of nothing, and is the owner of everything."

Upon these words of Yasfa everyone in the honor stand jumped up. Great amazement was being experienced there. Yasfa:

"Moses is not a magician, what he did is not magic, his words are true. Being of those who believe in him makes us proud. As for you, you are a liar. Do whatever you can to us, worldly life is no longer our concern."

These brave words, were the words of a sincere heart that wasn't after what it had lost after finding the truth. Murmuring was rising from the clearance that had been filled by Copts. A few tears ran from Sinuha's eyes:

"How fortunate are believers. These words are dripping from hearts that have tasted belief."

With a voice only her maid could hear, Asiya said:

"O Allah, what an elevated and sublime feeling belief is. How ordinary and low is the world for them."

Her maid held her hands crying:

"O Glorious Queen, I too want to believe in the god of Moses, that is Allah, prostrate to Him, and if necessary, die with honor like them for it."

"O my girl, as long as belief flows in one's soul, they will feel above all powers, they will despise and disregard tyrants torment. But you be quiet, and wait patiently."

Suddenly the voice of the magician of the northern districts was heard:

"O Pharaoh. Until now I thought being close to you was the biggest blessing on earth, that is what I was living for. However, Moses' staff beat our magic, showing the weakness of deception, we met true power. Now I believe in the God of Moses, Allah, Who created the sky and the earth. I shall not hold you above Allah."

The Prophets were shedding tears of joy.

It was Magician Azur's turn to have his say:

"O Pharaoh, you can only rule our world, however worldly life is short and worthless. The tortures you are considering for us do not express anything for our hearts we have submitted to Allah. We were expecting rewards from you when we won the contest, however we learned from Moses that the reward given by Allah is both very precious and eternal."

The magician of the water snake district:

"O Pharaoh, claiming that we have political motives is ridiculous. The only cause of our act is believing in the Divine Being Moses told about."

Yasfa's voice was heard again:

"You don't believe these claims yourself, you are only trying to confuse the people, to stop them believing in the truth."

The Pharaoh was stunned from listening to the accusations. He wanted to say something, but he couldn't.

The magician of the crocodile district:

"You want to take revenge from us for believing in miracles, we are not afraid of your threatening."

Sinuha was so excited, he was shaking:

"Father. The Pharaoh is helpless in the face of the magicians believing, his tyranny that he thought ruled hearts is defeated against believing hearts. If a heart wants to reach Allah, what can tyranny do to it?"

"Surprising, isn't it? Those expecting rewards and position from the Pharaoh, and those despising his threats and accepting death are the same people."

The crocodile district magician's "We're not afraid of your threats" rebellion had driven the Pharaoh crazy. He roared as if he had lost his mind:

"Take these ungrateful away."

Upon the Pharaoh's order the Amun troops securing the clearance brutally attacked the magicians that were either praying or prostrating, begging for forgiveness. They started to swing the thick batons in their hands on the old magicians without mercy. While they were all being dragged on the ground in blood, Yasfa was shouting at the top of his voice:

"O Allah, give us patience, and take our lives as believers."

The sound of magicians shouting "Allah" was ringing out in the clearance. The Egyptian people had fled in fear. A little later only the Prophets were left in front of the stand.

The way the Pharaoh wildly treated the magicians put Sinuha and his father in deep sorrow. Sinuha said:

"The Pharaoh knows that one cannot believe in two gods at the same time, one must be chosen. In the case of the people selecting the Lord of Moses his authority will be destroyed, his reign will be ruined. That is why he is terrified. Even the idolater magicians that took the Pharaoh as god until now turned away from him, they prostrated in front of everyone and believed in the Lord of Moses."

"Yes son, that is why the Pharaoh doesn't want to allow the people to freely believe in Allah. He thinks he can prevent them following Moses by using violence like this."

"He can't stop it."

Do You Think Your Dead Will Be Eternal by Mummifying Them

The people of Egypt had heard that the magicians, the foundation of the Pharaoh's regime, had believed in the Lord of Moses despite all threats, and had fallen into a serious dilemma. The Amun priests who had entered the religion of Moses had been thrown in dungeons, left hungry there for days and whipped with hemp fiber because of their belief in Allah. The priests whose right hands and left feet were chopped off with executioners' axes upon the second order of the Pharaoh were left to die painfully for hours, and then hung on gallows set up on the shore of the Nile. It had horrified the people.

Although the miracles shown by the Prophets to prove their claims were very clear, because of the management's violent policy, very few people could believe in them. And these were a hybrid generation whose mothers were Israelites and fathers were Copts. These young people weren't subject to the utter suppression as the full blooded children of the Israelites because they were half Copt, their different position was protecting them from being crushed to a certain degree. However, even these youngsters were suspicious of the evil of selfish people, they were afraid of flatterers like Korah cooperating with the Pharaoh and squealing on them. Especially the violent policy that Korah, the governor of Goshen, who was of Israelite descent applied to his nation was worrying everybody. Korah was closely following both Moses and his young supporters, and was reporting their activities day by day to the palace, requesting serious precautions to be taken. In this phase, they needed very strong faith to refresh their hearts and give them stamina against dangers they were likely to face. Although, lately it could be felt that the regime had softened noticeably. Arrests had decreased, torture and oppression had stopped, and a surprising period of improvement had begun. However, everyone evaluated this as the calm before the storm, and nobody could trust the Pharaoh.

* * *

The Pharaoh, gathered his staff in the orange mansion, he had called them for a special meeting. Ramesses, sitting on his dazzling golden throne pompously, turned to the Goshen governor Korah and said:

"Tell me, what's going on around Moses? We left them alone for a long time, we didn't oppress them, and we watched them from a distance. We didn't want to instigate Moses gaining followers or sharpen their attitude against the regime by oppressing the youngsters. We didn't want our people to think that we were afraid of his thoughts and that we are helpless against his ideas. We thought these wrong ideas would fade away in time by themselves. The reason for us leaving Moses alive was to show our people that we didn't take him or his ideas seriously."

"O mighty Emperor, your policy on the Israelites has worked well. There aren't many people around Moses, but they are slowly growing in numbers. The developments could cause a serious danger not now but in the future."

The Pharaoh corrected his blue crown, the symbol of his reign:

"Are you trying to say that Moses is respected?"

"His influence on the youngsters is increasing. Accepting you as god and respecting your statues isn't taken seriously."

"My statues represent me."

"They prefer a Lord who is known through the reflections of His power on the universe to your statues."

With a loud voice Ramesses said:

"Nonsense!"

Haman broke the short silence. Opening his eyes as wide as he could:

"Did we release Moses so that he could announce to everyone that his God is Lord, and so they could turn away from you and our gods? They are saying that the order on earth belongs to Allah; they want to overthrow our regime, and abolish our system that is based on you being god."

Korah interrupted:

"Whereas Egypt takes its power from its gods, and accepts you as their beloved child."

The Grand Vizier's voice was heard again:

"Moses deserting our gods and worshiping his own god, is our foundations that we take strength from crumbling."

Board members nodded their heads to confirm.

The words of Haman and Korah had both upset Ramesses, and made him understand the reaction against the regime. The footsteps of an order that was going to abolish the Pharaoh regime could be heard.

The Pharaoh raised his scepter and silenced all in the lounge. His face was tense, his eyes were full of hate:

"Haman. Execute those who believe in the God of Moses, cut off the hands and feet of the ringleaders and throw them to the crocodiles."

The grand vizier was delighted:

"As you wish representative of Horus."

"Leave the women alive."

"As you wish."

"Everyone shall know that we are strong enough to crush our enemies."

Applause rose from the board.

The Israelites had suffered similar wild methods in the years that Moses was born. The men being brutally murdered, the women being left alive at the mercy of the Copts, it was difficult times at the beginning of the Prophethood period, but what could be done, this was the method of disbelief against belief throughout history.

Prince Sinuha murmured "Tyranny."

Imhotep leaned over and whispered in to his ear:

"Please son, it is time to be patient."

After greeting the Pharaoh by prostrating, Haman said:

"O child of the gods, your decision will make our country rejoice."

The Goshen Governor Korah:

"Moses being alive could cause a rebellion."

Once again Sinuha couldn't stop himself:

"Scum" he said, and was about to stand up to advance upon the governor.

His father invited him to patience again:

"Benefit doesn't recognize blood ties; it speaks every language and takes every form" he whispered, and then talked to his brother, the Pharaoh:

"O Great Savior that protected our country from invasion. Killing Moses will not solve the problem, on the contrary it will raise him to being a saint, and increase the interest in his religion. Killing Moses will feed the fire of rebellion. I find such a decision dangerous for our future."

Justice Minister Hennu:

"If Moses is killed, his God could attempt to take revenge on us. Let's leave him alone."

Haman began to speak:

"He wants to stir up Egypt."

Sinuha stood up all of a sudden and shouted:

"You are who is stirring up Egypt, you are slandering Moses."

A discussion started among the board, everybody was saying something else. Looking at Sinuha with a grudge, Haman said:

"Moses must be killed, and by torture" he hissed.

This request caused disturbance among the nobles. The rulers thought that it would get worse with the killing of Moses. Sinuha was determined to talk despite his father who was trying to stop him:

"O noble Uncle" he said to start with.

All eyes were on him. He was both a good speech maker and the nephew of the Pharaoh. He was the most influential name after Haman, he was the treasurer. The grand vizier made a sour face and prepared to listen to him. Korah's lips were turned down.

"Are you going to kill a human just because he says 'Allah is my Lord'? Can a person be killed for an expression of his personal belief, his personal conviction? What a disgusting judgment. What happened to the justice that made Egypt great? We know that our forefathers said that god hates those who are single sided. If we are afraid and skeptical about every word of someone, what kind of justice is this? (Looking at Haman) A vizier's mission is to be upright and fair. Didn't our forefathers say 'Do not add your pride into your knowledge, do not be conceited because of your knowledge, take advice from the ignorant as much as you do from intellectuals. If you are in a high position, wish well for all. Being correct is the highest achievement in life '?"

Turning to Korah:

"Don't be ambitious for a fortune, this is an incurable illness, the source of all that is reprehensible."

To the board members:

"Dear members, the famous philosopher Ani says 'Words ruin a person, do not say wrong things.' Refrain from making wrong decisions."

He waited for a few seconds, he looked at the members carefully:

"When Moses said 'Allah is my Lord' he showed evidence too. If he was lying by saying 'Allah wants you to worship Him, He wants you to abandon the gods you believe in.', his words will cause results in adverse, let's wait and he shall bear the consequences. Attempting to kill him for it will not justify us, but if he is telling the truth, the punishment he is threatening with will find us. Let's refrain from being excessive against Moses and his Lord. If the punishment of Allah comes, who will take it away from us, who will help us? Won't we all be weak and helpless before His punishment?"

Everybody was listening to his words in curiosity.

"Weren't the magicians beaten by the miracle of Moses and left helpless? Didn't they all say 'This is not magic, it is a miracle'? However they were killed. Doesn't all of this tell you anything? I am a Copt too, one of you, a piece of this community, a member of the regime. I do not see myself different to you, but I am concerned about the future of Egypt."

The Pharaoh who realized Sinuha had begun to influence the listeners raised his staff and didn't allow him to finish his words.

"O Nobles, I show you the truth. Only what I say is the truth, do not seek any truth other than it."

Minister İmhotep murmured:

"He can't even stand it being implied that he could make a mistake. Can't an opinion different from his be told? Does everything said by dictators have to be right?"

Prince Sinuha murmured:

"If he respected other thoughts and listened to different ideas he wouldn't be one of those in denial."

The Pharaoh's words had been welcomed by Haman with joy. He had smiled so wide that his rotting teeth had appeared with all their ugliness.

"We are always your followers, followers of our forefathers," he shouted.

Sinuha was determined to say what he thought whatever the price would be. It was the day to take sides with Moses. He wasn't going to resign from conveying the message, he was going to try to enter the hearts of the board members in a different way. He wanted to attract their attention to nations that lived in the past, and Prophets who conveyed the message to them. Softening the tone of his voice:

"O Noble Uncle, and noble members. Do you not know about the disasters that happened to the people of Noah, Ad, Thamud and other denying nations that came after them? Those who denied Prophet Noah were destroyed by a flood, they were swept away by the flood and died. Those who attacked Prophet Hud were destroyed by a strong wind. Those who didn't recognize Prophet Saleh were destroyed with an earthquake. Allah does not oppress people, but he does punish those who torment believers, takes away their powers and wipes them off the face of the earth. Give up tyrannizing Moses. I am afraid of a calamity that could find our nation, aren't you?"

Asiya was moved. She had noticed something different about both Moses and Sinuha, she had treated them with compassion since they were children, as if they were her own children. Now she was crying, seeing that she wasn't wrong, and her efforts had given results. She was praying to her Lord for Him to protect Moses and Sinuha from the Pharaoh's tyranny.

As Moses did, Sinuha too told about Allah having infinite knowledge, and that the punishment and torment in the hereafter was worse than it was on earth:

"On the Day of Judgment screams will mix with each other, I am not capable to tell the terrible sight at Armageddon. If you are to kill Moses, those that you are following will not be able to save you on that horrendous day when everybody will be trying to save themselves from the torment of hell. Nobody will be found to help you against Allah on that day."

Looking at Ubiante, the chief commander of the Ptah armies, who was listening to him arrogantly with his medals shining on his chest:

"Tyrants who patronize based on their worldly positions, and those who are preparing to tyrannize believers based on their power will not be pitied in the hereafter."

The face of Ubiante, who had been in competition with Sinuha about Princess Tiye from the beginning, had turned yellow like beeswax, his hand went to his sword. Imhotep was in a cold sweat; his hands were as cold as ice. Even if he was his nephew, could Ramesses stand such harsh criticism? He was shaking for his only son, worried about his brother's anger which had hung the most famous magicians in the country with a single order on the shore of the Nile. Sinuha had openly set forth his belief in Moses and his Lord. Now he had no friends in this assembly. But Sinuha was thinking that if Moses was to be killed his mission would suffer, and that he had to help him even if it cost his own life. The die had been cast already. Aiming at Korah:

"Even his own nation doesn't support him, just like his forefathers did to Prophet Joseph. Just as their forefathers doubted Prophet Joseph who came to them with clear miracles, now his nation is continuing the same attitude towards Moses. Whereas he is a Prophet confirming what Prophet Joseph had said. The dignitaries of this nation are following the bad path of their forefathers. When Prophet Joseph died his nation said 'Allah won't send another Prophet,' but He has. Divine Power definitely punishes those who are doubtful about believing despite the clear proof that came to them."

Sinuha had put the cat among the pigeons by talking like Moses. He finished his words saying:

"Harming Moses will cause you trouble."

After greeting the Pharaoh respectfully, he calmly sat down. All eyes were on the Pharaoh. Was Moses going to be killed? What kind of punishment was awaiting Sinuha? When Ramesses sat up in his throne among the surprised looks of the board members, everybody stood up.

"O Nobles of my Country. Sinuha doesn't think like us, but he spoke so bravely and sincerely that I shall not punish him. And Moses will not be killed for now."

The Pharaoh was not accepting to believe in Allah despite all the efforts of the Young Prince, he was insisting in his denial. However his proof he put forward was so convincing that Ramesses had to take notice of it. Then in a sarcastic manner:

"Haman. Build me a high, very high tower. I shall climb its stairs to reach the sky and maybe I will talk with the God of Moses there," he said.

The Young Prince quietly whispered:

"You are forcing yourself to denial, you are talking nonsense."

The Pharaoh was continuing his revolt:

"I shall seek him in the sky and find him."

Smiles were spreading through the lounge. Gritting his teeth the Young Prince said:

"Your reign will totally collapse."

"Haman. Light a big fire, and then burn the bricks fine. I want a high, very high tower."

The lounge was rocking with laughter.

Imhotep invited his son to patience once again:

"I don't think he believes what he is saying, he's trying to save his pride."

Smiling with his dirty teeth Haman said:

"Your wish is an order, O Child of the gods."

The Pharaoh became serious all of a sudden, turning to Sinuha:

"Moses says that a Lord in the sky sent him, I shall prove his words are groundless."

Moses being accused with telling lies had made the prince angry.

Minister İmhotep whispered:

"Don't answer, he's trying to agitate you."

He wasn't afraid of anyone, and was only worried about Moses' life:

"Worldly life isn't eternal, but the hereafter is eternal. Moses is telling the truth, showing the true path."

Seriousness was back in the lounge.

"Those who do evil in this world will be punished in the hereafter, those who do good deeds will be rewarded."

The screechy voice of Pontiff Unas was heard:

"Sinuha should apologize to our gods."

"O Poor Unas, I am inviting you to felicity, you are inviting me to fire. You are considering the dreams you believe in and Allah equal. You believe that Oziris who you accept as the god of the afterlife will take the form of a dog and protect you. By mummifying your dead you think they will live eternally like that. You assume a poor black bull as a symbol of the gods, and try to make divine meanings out of its every move. Can't you understand that an unconscious and helpless animal cannot be a god? Dividing the Lord's power among make believe gods is a lie of magicians. You accept stars, bulls, dogs, jackals, crocodiles, vultures, snakes and even an ordinary insect as a god. What heedlessness!"

After taking a deep breath:

"O Poor Unas, are you expecting me to accept unconscious creatures as a god?"

Asiya walked towards the exit with slow steps. Her heart couldn't take Sinuha's brave defense anymore. As the door decorated with vine patterns was closing behind her she heard the prince's last sentence:

"There's no difference between inviting to denial and inviting to fire."

After telling the guards not to follow her, the old Queen walked towards the copse covered with trees. She could smell the wonderful fragrance of soil and trees.

She was worn out in the last few years. Her hair was turning gray, wrinkles had appeared on her face. Despite the storm of denial around her she always believed, resisted fearlessly in the palace of the tyrant king, in this ocean of disbelief she had always opened her hands to her owner. But she was exhausted, now the palace of the Pharaoh was like a dungeon for her.

The Nile was shining like silver with the last rays of light. She dropped herself on the green leaves and colorful flowers. The tears running from her eyes fell on the pink flowers like drops of dew. Opening her hands to the sky, she repeated her usual prayer:

"O Helper of the helpless, save me from the Pharaoh's tyranny, give me a place in your heaven."

The queen's prayer was an example of her not caring about worldly blessings. For, she was the wife of the most powerful king on earth; she could get the most precious of what she desired whenever she wanted, but she was putting all of this aside and asking her Lord for salvation.

This Tyranny Will Happen to People in the Future Too

As the smell of oak and hornbeam was spreading from the forest, and the last rays of the sun lit up the hills covered with flowers, a beautiful view that one couldn't get enough of came alive. It was a spring evening that filled hearts with the joy of life, however the Israelites were in fear. Sinuha had sent a message for them to be careful. Moses combed his hair which was turning gray with his fingers. He was smiling as usual with compassion. Natal broke the silence:

"Yesterday, all the men of the Ammonites were hung on the shore of the Nile. They cut off the right hands and left feet of the youngsters and left them to die. The tongues of the youngsters of Rahal have been cut off because they wouldn't say 'We are the Pharaoh's followers.'"

Prophet Moses:

"Brothers, the world is Allah's property. The Pharaoh and his nation are guests on this property. The owner of the world has defined when to send them off his property, and fixated the day of fate. Believers don't think that tyrant idolaters will put down roots in this world, and will not imagine that it is impossible for them to be destroyed. Our brothers died for Allah, they are martyrs; they won Paradise. Let us be patient against calamity, the help of our Lord is close."

Young Ahod began to speak:

"O Messenger of Allah, one night ago Uncle Hilyod's house was raided. His sons, sons in law and grandsons were taken away. The dungeons of Memphis are shattering with the cries of Israelite children."

"O servants of Allah! Do not allow death to scare you, do not allow your hearts to be shaken by the horror of the events. Death is not nothingness, it is merely a change of place. For believers, the life after death is felicity. Those who believe in Allah are going to win this war."

Another youngster said:

"Let's go before our turn comes."

Staying calm, Prophet Moses said:

"Let's be patient so that our Lord will come to our rescue. Believers don't hurry; because they can't see behind the curtain of human perception, they don't know what is better for them. Let's ask for His help."

* * *

This time tyranny had started very violently. The tongues and ears of those who said "Allah" were being cut off, their lips were pierced, their fingers were broken, their flesh was cut; people were being thrown into fire alive. The believers who had run out of patience were complaining to the Prophet. An old Israelite said:

"O Moses, your coming didn't change anything; we suffered before you, and after you. We don't know when our pain will end."

Moses spoke determinedly:

"This tyranny happened to people before us, and it will happen to people in the future too. The war with disbelief will go on till the Day of Judgment."

Two people hiding their faces with striped covers entered the group. A little later the younger one lifted the cover on his face.

Moses smiled and said:

"Welcome, but I haven't seen you before."

"We come from far away, from the other side of Goshen, the shore of the Red Sea."

"Your name?"

"Abigail."

"I think I've heard this name before. It's usually used for girls."

"My grandfather named me, in the memory of his grandchild that was burned."

Moses trembled.

"Or is your grandfather's name Ezekiel?"

The old man took off his cover too. Amazed, Moses said:

"You are Ezekiel's son Abel."

He jumped up and hugged Abel.

"Is your father alive?"

"No, Messenger of Allah, it has been five years since he passed away."

"He changed my life, I believe he is within Allah's mercy."

Turning to the crowd Moses said:

"Brothers, the foundation of belief is trusting Allah. The biggest force that increases the resistance of a weak and minority community against a tyrant regime is trusting Him. Surrender yourselves to Allah."

Young Abigail:

"We take refuge in our Lord."

A youngster with flashing eyes:

"So do we."

Someone else:

"O Allah, do not test us with tyrants."

Natal:

"Have mercy for us, save us from the tyranny of disbelievers O Lord."

* * *

Every night, they were gathering in one of the adobe cottages hidden behind high walls, they would raise their hands to the sky altogether and start to pray.

The voice of Prophet Moses rose among the crowd:

"Believers don't want calamity, but when they encounter it they must be patient."

Altogether they said:

"We are with you till death, we'll give our lives for you."

"Brothers, the most powerful weapon in war is belief. At the moment of severity the weapon in disbelievers' hands is of no use. Now I am going to ask you to do something. Cut all your ties with the Copts."

Young Ahod:

"What do you mean?"

"Leave the rotten Copts alone, separate from them. Do not go to their temples, do not worship their idols, do not join their festivals. Prepare for war until Allah's good tidings come."

Looking over the crowd:

"Make your homes' a mosque, glorify Allah there, offer prayers, and memorize the verses of the Torah. Spread these words of mine among our nation."

"O Prophet, the rich Copts trick some of us with their fortunes. Those whose nature isn't that strong lose themselves in the face of their richness and want to be like them, and subject to them."

Moses hadn't answered this question. Because it was late, the believers quietly went their own ways. Allah's Messenger had given up on the Pharaoh. He raised his hands to the sky and wished guidance to the Copt nation. And then he begged to his Lord:

"O Lord, you gave the Pharaoh and his nation worldly goods. The Copts are taking advantage of this richness to trick our nation. Unaware of these blessings being a test, the Israelites are falling under its spell. My wish from You is that You destroy the fortune in the hands of this tyrant power, squeeze their hearts. They are not going to believe without experiencing Your burning torment."

Aaron was joining in, saying "Amen", to the prayers of Moses. Their prayers and glorification went on till dawn. After a long silence they found peace with a revelation that came to their hearts.

"Your prayers have been accepted."

Water Turning to Blood Is Very Different to Other Disasters

*E*ight years had passed after the contest between Moses and the magicians, the belief mission in the Israelite neighborhoods in Goshen had expanded. Lessons from the Torah were continuing secretly in houses, those who subjected to Moses were increasing.

The lesson that night was in Prophet Moses' cottage. Allah's Messenger was describing belief:

"Brothers, belief is both light and power. A believer who attains true belief can challenge the universe and can be saved from drowning among the waves of events which are as big as mountains. Belief gives us happiness in both this world and in the hereafter. Everything is subject to knowledge. The source of all knowledge is knowing Allah, and then believing in Him."

The lesson had finished. The youngsters took a few dates from the earthenware pot. Young Abigail said:

"Dear Prophet, it has been raining nonstop for ten days in the Nile reservoir, it's raining cats and dogs. All Egypt is under water, hundreds of people died in floods, thousands of animals perished, lands became lakes. There isn't a single piece of food left in the houses of the Copts."

Natal started to speak:

"Our Dear Prophet. We are witnessing a miracle. The earth is swallowing the flood water before it reaches Goshen. The clouds are flying over us without causing any damage; but the Copts aren't giving up their stubbornness despite these clear miracles, they are continuing to deny, they can't see the Divine Power behind the calamity. The comments of the Amun priests concentrate on causes."

Abel, one of the elders of the community:

"Unfortunately the magicians and the Copts can't establish a connection between the events and the Messenger of Allah."

Yasfa's son Sharim:

"The Nile overflowed so much this year that everywhere is under water. There isn't the smallest piece of land left to cultivate. Even Imhotep can't find a solution for this problem."

At that moment, Gershom, the son of Prophet Moses came to the porch lit by torches and said:

"Father, a noble from the palace wants to see you."

"Send him in."

An old, short, plump man who had lost most of his hair appeared at the door. He was wearing plain clothes.

"Greetings to you, the Glorious Leader of the Israelites. I am Kabahu, the Governor of the White Wall District. I bring you the greetings of Pharaoh Ramesses, I came to you with a request in the name of my nation. The endless heavy showers left our plains and fields flooded, and destroyed our crops. Our people died, our animals perished. The Nile overflowed into our houses and gardens, we have nothing left to eat, famine has started in our country, our children are hungry and wretched. Our Pharaoh says: 'This is Moses' country too, tell him to pray to his Lord so that He can remove this terrible disaster from us. I promise we will not harm him anymore, I will even believe in his Lord with my nation.'"

The District Governor was quiet waiting for an answer. Moses asked:

"Is that all you have to say?"

"The Pharaoh will allow you to leave the country with your nation."

The Prophet looked at his old friend and asked:

"What do you say Abel?"

"The Pharaoh cannot be trusted. They had begged in previous storms too and made promises. Upon your prayers Allah had stopped the disasters. But after time passed they forgot their promises and denied everything. Didn't they even say that rain was a blessing for them, and that meadows in their towns had multiplied and their crops had increased?"

Rubbing his hands, Governor Kabahu said:

"This is a very different situation, the damage of the floods is unbearable. The other floods were suitable for the Nile's structure, the cultivation of Egypt had gained strength from them."

Young Sharim:

"When the Copts didn't hold up to their promises after the flood, Allah sent grasshoppers to warn them. One morning they woke up to see that the sun had been covered by a brownish cloud. Not long after a crowded population of grasshoppers landed in Egypt. These vicious gnawers covered the whole land like a cover of death, they destroyed all the crops. Nobody had ever seen anything like it before. Then an unbearable famine unfolded. They were helpless and they had come here again begging. They had said that if the calamity was lifted off them they would believe and they would set us free. You hadn't given up hope on them finding the true path and said that you would pray for them. So the grasshopper calamity too was lifted off them with the mercy of our Lord. However, the ungrateful idolaters didn't come to reason, they didn't believe in Allah."

Prophet Aaron looked at Sharim and smiled:

"The Copts who had to make a choice between the Lord of the Universe and the gods of their forefathers needed other miracles and their repetition."

The Governor was relieved by this statement which was in favor of the Copts, but he was still anxious:

"You will pray for us, won't you?" he asked.

Moses who saw Abigail losing his patience allowed him to speak:

"Once our Lord had sent the calamity of insects. The small, wingless grasshoppers were insistently eating every last bit of the crop, not leaving a single wheat kernel for the farmers. Also small bugs had multiplied, they were biting people all over, sucking their blood. The Copts were about to lose their minds. Finally they sent a mediator again, and begged for help. When the Glorious Prophet prayed the calamity was lifted off them. But the result didn't change, they didn't give up worshiping bulls or statues."

Sharim spoke again:

"Didn't the Pharaoh try to provoke the people against us by saying 'These calamities are caused by the curse of Moses and his followers' and blaming our Prophet for it after every flood and famine?"

Prophet Moses turned to the Governor and asked:

"What do you have to say to this?"

"I'm sorry powerful leader. As you know, I live far from Memphis, I didn't know about this. Please, pray for our babies that go to sleep hungry."

Moses' son Gershom:

"Do I have a say in this matter father?"

"Tell your opinion too!"

"It was the end of last year. Upon your prayers the grasshopper calamity had just been lifted off them. But once again they had sidestepped, and hadn't given up their idols. Then our Lord had sent frogs on them."

The youngsters started to laugh.

"Tens of thousands of frogs were filling streets, houses, pantries, storehouses, pots and even beds. Nobody could cast them out, the whole country was filled with frogs for days. These weird creatures pestered them so badly that if the people tried to sleep, or opened their mouth to talk, the frogs would try to get in to their mouth."

The laughter on the porch had turned to chuckling, the governor was regretting coming. Yasfa's son carried on:

"They came again, they requested the calamity to be lifted off them. And they didn't forget the lie that they would believe if the calamity was lifted off them."

Abigail smiled and said:

"As they do every time."

Abel:

"Lies, lies, and more lies."

The Governor didn't know what to say. Abel continued:

"The Prophet didn't give up hope that they might understand that these calamities are miracles of Divine Power and give up denying that time, so he prayed again. Finally they were saved from this calamity too. It was as if the frogs had been swallowed by the ground overnight. However, the ungrateful nation resisted in denying. They weren't believing the Compassionate Prophet who was trying to give them eternal felicity, and even insulting him."

Sharim added:

"We even heard that the Pharaoh said 'Whatever he does to charm us we will not believe in him, he is wasting his time with us.'"

Abel started to speak again:

"They are refusing to understand that all that happened to them were Divine signs to warn them off their wrong beliefs."

When Abel saw clouds of sorrow on the face of the Prophet he didn't beat about the bush:

"These calamities all came to the Copts. In Goshen there were no grasshoppers or frogs. Lice or fleas didn't bite us. We didn't suffer severe famine either. Why can't the Pharaoh understand this? Isn't it obvious who is on the true path? Don't they see the clear miracles?"

Aaron took over:

"Can't you see that the calamities that target the nation of the Pharaoh are causing the Israelites to connect to Moses?"

With sincere seriousness Moses said:

"Listen Dear Delegate, the Pharaoh's reign turned a deaf ear to the warnings that showed Allah has mercy for

His servants every time. Despite all, for the innocent I shall beg to my Lord again. Please be our guest tonight."

Happiness could be seen on the Governor's face. After greeting the Prophet by bending over almost to the ground he quietly left the porch. As not a single drop of rain was falling in Goshen the darkness on the horizon was being lit up by lightning striking again and again.

* * *

Three months had passed since Governor Kabahu visited Moses. The storm had passed, Egypt had started to dress its wounds of the floods. As the sun was preparing to light up the world again the Prophets were surrounded by youngsters as usual. Prophet Moses finished his morning lesson with these words:

"Nobody can totally satisfy their desires with the pleasures of this world. Those wonderful things that are created, are to direct people to draw a lesson and feel gratitude. They are samples of the real blessings that our Lord has prepared in Paradise for believers."

Young Abigail:

"Were all beauties created for eternity?"

"All of our Lord's art is for eternity, they face eternity. For example, look at this exceptional smelling rose. As soon as its mission is completed it will die. But its beauties will remain in the memories of people who saw it."

Sharim jumped up and said:

"In that case humans aren't aimless either."

"That's right Sharim, humans aren't abandoned. All of their acts in this world are watched and recorded. All of our words and acts are preserved. When the time comes, we will answer for them in the presence of Allah, and either be rewarded or punished."

Prophet Aaron:

"Another life after death is just like spring coming after winter."

Gershom who had just come to the porch:

"Father, the Treasurer is here."

"Bring him in, I'm coming."

Allah's Messengers went to the room overlooking the garden.

"Welcome Dear Friend."

"Thank you."

Sinuha slowly removed the striped cover that only left his eyes open off his head. There was hope and loyalty in his Nile blue looks.

"I missed you."

"As you know, successive famines ruined our economy. However they don't want to understand that Allah's power is behind it all. Their minds are in their eyes. They can't comprehend anything beyond what is seen. Their feelings are stiff, their hearts are blind."

Prophet Aaron added:

"Whereas there are no coincidences in the universe."

Moses started to speak again:

"I was hoping the blood miracle would have directed them to awakening."

Prince Sinuha:

"All the waters in creeks, wells, and in containers all suddenly turned into blood. That day the Pharaoh was terrified, he said 'Go to Moses immediately, request him to pray to his Lord.'"

"After every calamity he sends one of his viziers and says 'The Pharaoh wants you to pray to your Lord. If he lifts this calamity off us we will believe in Him, we will allow the Israelites to leave with you.' I had prayed to our Lord then too, and He lifted that blood calamity which lasted seven days off them. However, they didn't keep their promises once again."

"Their arrogance is preventing them, Dear Prophet."

"Water turning to blood is a miracle very different to other disasters. The blood calamity had targeted water, that is people directly. In that perspective it was expected to convince them. After that miracle the Copts should have made the right choice."

Prophet Aaron:

"The people of Egypt run to Moses when they are in trouble, they request him to lift the calamity off them, but they don't accept to believe in Allah."

Sinuha confirmed what Aaron said:

"You are right. The Pharaoh is making an exceptional effort for the right information to not reach the people. The regime prefers to take all miracles as results of natural events, deny and make the people deny Allah's power. They underestimate miracles, they even make fun of them. For this reason, even if miracles shock people, due to the regime, soon everything is considered normal. But the Copts are guilty too. Because they are aware that miracles are made by Allah, but they obey the Pharaoh with their own free will, not being able to overcome their pride. 'Are we to believe ordinary people whose nation are our slaves?' they say."

"How do you see the future?"

"The system claims that calamities happened because of bad luck. They are trying to make the people believe that these events happened because of you and your followers. However, as long as your services to faith continue their propaganda will lose effect. Underestimating miracles, making fun of them, even the increase of violence will not be able to prevent belief in Allah spreading. Especially after the blood miracle, even among the nobles a great transformation is happening. I have a surprise for you."

"Don't make us curious, tell us."

"I heard that Goshen Governor Korah, a strict follower of the Pharaoh, wants to subject to you."

The Prophets smiled in joy.

"I even heard the Pharaoh saying 'I have strength and power, however Moses...' in an important meeting last week, comparing himself with you who he didn't make anything of for years."

Prophet Moses raised his hands and thanked his Lord, then with a loud voice he said:

"O Pharaoh, I believe you will perish, and your nation are criminals and sinners."

Then, with a sad voice:

"Dear Friend, has Mother Asiya's death been demystified?"

"We don't know anything but that she was found dead in her bed. But she was ill lately, and she was tired of the Pharaoh's oppression. In one of our conversations she said 'Son, I beg to my Lord at dawn for Him to save me from this denying nation.' Then tears ran from her eyes like rain, she raised her hands and prayed: 'O Allah, reserve a place for me too in Your Paradise.' We both prayed and then I left. The following morning it was announced that she was found dead in her bed."

"Could the Pharaoh or Haman have done any evil?"

"There is nothing to prove such a thing, but all evil can be expected from them."

The Prophets bowed their heads and prayed for mother Asiya, they wished her Allah's mercy.

Sinuha asked for permission to leave and stood up. As he always did, he wrapped his head in the striped cover. His Nile blue eyes were shining with hope among the cover.

As Moses was seeing Sinuha off, he quietly asked:

"Is there any news from Tiye?"

The brightness in the Prince's eyes decreased:

"A voice inside me says that she is still alive. I still love her, I am patiently waiting for the day that I will rejoin her."

Sinuha jumped on the white horse awaiting him in the courtyard and pulled away as a villager.

My Aim Is to Completely Annihilate the Israelites

The Cabinet meeting was being held in the dazzlingly beautiful Green Mansion. The bright colored seats in the large lounge had been filled by commanders and priests along with ministers. A nauseating fragrance was spreading from the flowers in the elegant vases. The Pharaoh was sitting in his gold gilded throne loftily, with his red crown on his head, looking around arrogantly. The usual merciless look was on his face.

Grand Vizier Haman opened the meeting. He had put his apricot yellow cape over his shoulders:

"Great Ramesses, the Noble Representative of Powerful Horus. Our forefathers said 'Greetings to you O Nile, to give life to Egypt you come from far away, and give life to the thirsty.' however we have been struggling with famine for years. The Nile doesn't overflow anymore. There is no wheat, no corn, nothing, our fields are dry and our granaries are empty. The water of the Faiyum Dam is almost completely gone, the people are hungry and wretched. Because the gods turned away from us."

The Pharaoh turned his dark looks to Sinuha:

"How about our treasury?"

"The Grand Vizier is telling the truth. The Nile hasn't overflowed for years, news of drought and hunger is coming from all over the country. We reduced the taxes on farmers, our treasury is melting day by day. If we take the farmers subsistence wheat and corn seeds it will be worse next year."

The Pharaoh jumped up in anger:

"The bad luck of Moses and his nation is the cause of all the calamities that happened."

Ramesses couldn't continue. For Vizier Hesepti who had entered through the door had moved towards him in panic. After prostrating in front of the golden throne he greeted the king respectfully.

The Pharaoh:

"What's going on Hesepti, why are you panicking?"

"They are leaving."

"In the name of Ra, speak clearly, who is going where?"

"The Israelites my King; they are leaving Egypt with their horses, carts, and all their animals. They are heading towards the Red Sea, following Moses."

The Pharaoh roared in dismay:

"With whose permission?"

Sinuha answered with a dignified voice:

"Yours mighty Pharaoh."

"What do you mean?"

"Three months ago you had said that they could leave if they ended the plague."

The Pharaoh turned to Vizier Hesepti and asked:

"Where are they?"

"They are four days from Memphis. They are proceeding towards the Red Sea from the end of Etham Desert. They have taken plenty of water and provisions with them. It is clear that they have planned this escape well in advance."

"Haman. How did they get that far?"

"O Glorious god, when the plague ended an old man by the name of Abel asked for your permission to celebrate collectively at a place three days from Memphis and you allowed them. Since that day the Israelites have been gathering in groups in the wetlands at the end of Etham Desert, in the delta between Memphis and Pi Ramesses. Or have you forgotten?"

"I hadn't guessed that they would attempt such a thing."

Haman opened his eyes in fear:

"What do you order Glorious Master?"

"They can't proceed north or to the west, their only destination is the Red Sea. We do not need to hurry, they can't move fast, only one day is sufficient for us to catch up with them. That means we have five days to prepare."

After thinking for a short while, he said:

"Tell Ubiante to prepare his cavalry for battle, we shall leave on the fifth day. And you prepare a crowded army."

"Oh Great god! We are in a difficult situation due to the calamities that came one after another, it isn't easy to bring together a crowded army. Besides, the Israelites aren't crowded, and they could be considered unarmed. It won't be difficult."

A treacherous light momentarily shone in the Pharaoh's eyes:

"I know they are not to be feared. But my aim isn't to turn Moses around, I shall totally abolish the Israelites, wipe them off the face of the earth. I want Moses and Aaron alive."

Sinuha murmured to himself:

"You aren't afraid of Moses, you are afraid of his Lord."

The Pharaoh shouted out:

"Do not be afraid, they are a rubbish minority."

Haman leaned over to Pontiff Unas:

"He's getting too old, he doesn't know what he is saying. If they are a rubbish minority why do we need so many soldiers?"

The Pharaoh called out to his son Meneptah:

"I will go with the army. You shall stay here and deputize for me."

The Pharaoh's eyes were seeking the Goshen governor:

"Where is Korah?"

The ministers looked at each other worried. One of them said:

"Master, he is with Moses."

"What do you mean?"

"He was an Israelite."

"He will pay for his treason."

"He gathered his fortune days before and left."

"Sinuha believes in the god of Moses, but he is with us."

Vizier Hesepti:

"Noble god, there is another weird situation."

Ramesses frowned.

"This much weirdness is enough."

"The Israelites borrowed jewelry from Copt families. Gold, bracelets, necklaces, rings, everything that comes to mind."

Minister Athothis added:

"Clothes, thousands of loincloths and sandals."

"Why?"

"They said they were to wear at the festival."

Grand Vizier:

"It is obvious that they have done this just to make us believe that they will return to Memphis. They must have decided to leave Egypt a long time ago."

Vizier Hesepti:

"And some Copts were forced to lend their possessions."

"What do you mean?"

"Some Copt families went to Moses to ask him to help them be saved from the plague. And he said that he would help them in return for lending their jewelry. He put forward this condition for them to be saved."

"He tricked our people. As you can see, Moses is a liar."

Upset, Sinuha turned to his father and quietly said:

"The Pharaoh has lied to Moses many times in the past ten years. Whenever they were in trouble he promised to believe, whenever they were in hardship he said he would allow them to leave Egypt."

Raising his voice the Pharaoh said:

"Tell our brave soldiers that they haven't gone alone, that they have taken their belongings and their fortunes with them. If they want to regain their lost dignity and the jewelry, they should fight with great courage."

He shouted at the top of his voice, spitting grudge and hatred:

"Wait for me Moses. I am coming to beat you and your Lord."

They Started to Walk In
the Red Sea with Slow Steps

The Israelites had set off the midnight following Allah ordering Moses to migrate. They had been walking for days as a flood of people with their belongings and animals that they could take with them, they had been struggling in the heat of Etham Desert for five days. The sun was scorching everything, not even allowing them to catch their breath.

They were close to the Red Sea. Abel whipped his horse and approached Moses.

"O Allah's Messenger, there is a caravan approaching our convoy from the west."

The Prophet was calm:

"Let them come."

A little later horsemen with their head wrapped in striped covers got close. The leading horseman dismounted his white horse and took off his head cover.

Prophet Moses joyfully shouted:

"Sinuha!"

Worry could be seen in the blue eyes of the young Prince.

"We don't have any time to lose. The Pharaoh is after you with hundreds of chariots and thousands of cavalry. Because they know you are heading towards the Red Sea they aren't worried about you getting away. I secretly left before sunrise to tell you that you are being followed. The small amount of soldiers that you see are believers, and they are ready to die for you. However they are too small a unit to put up against Ramesses' army. The Pharaoh will be here in a few hours."

Sinuha was looking over the Prophet in suspicion, trying to catch a glance of hope in his looks.

Moses smiled and put his hand on his altruistic friends shoulder:

"Don't worry, Allah is with us. He wanted us to trust Him. We shall keep going."

A happy smile spread across Sinuha's face too.

"Listen my friend, when we were leaving the festival grounds I knew the Pharaoh could not be trusted, but I hoped he wouldn't follow us. Because the plague had taken the lives of thousands of Copts young and old. Then, they had come in groups, and begged for days for the calamity to be lifted off them; and the Pharaoh had sent word that we could leave the country straight away if we wished. This time I thought I could take his word for it. However, my Lord informed me that it was time to leave, that we should leave at night without being noticed, to walk towards the sea and that the Pharaoh's army would come after us."

"The Pharaoh said that you collected jewelry from the people saying that you would give it back."

"We did that to make them think we would come back."

"O Messenger of Allah! The Pharaoh isn't coming to take you back, he is coming to annihilate you all, young and old."

"I know."

When they made their way past the red sand dunes the Red Sea appeared. Under the sun, it was shining like a diamond. Abel's horse stopped close to Moses kicking up dust. His chestnut horse's hooves had sunk in the sand, it was in a sweat. He shouted excitedly:

"There is a small group approaching from the north."

"Are they the leading force of the Pharaoh's army?"

"No, there are women among them too."

"Bring them here straight away."

A little later Abel had come with the men with their heads wrapped up to the side of Moses who was having a sweet conversation with Sinuha. The Prophet asked:

"Who are you?"

When the stranger took off his head cover they were both surprised:

"What, Sepi!"

Sepi who they hadn't seen for twenty years and they thought had died in the war was standing in front of them. They hugged each other in tears. Sinuha broke the long silence:

"So you are alive!"

"I've been through a lot Sinuha."

"Your hair has turned gray."

"Just like yours."

They all laughed.

Sinuha said:

"Just like in our academy days, wonderful."

They hugged again.

Sinuha said:

"Where were you?"

"I had taken refuge in Asur. I heard of Moses' prophecy there and became a believer. My men notified me that you were coming towards the Red Sea a few days ago. We set off right away. We have been riding our horses for five days to catch up with you. We changed our guise not to be caught by the Haman beast."

Turning to Prophet Moses:

"O Messenger of Allah, O Dear Prophet! I can see that you are taking your nation towards the Red Sea. But forget a ship, not even a rowboat can be seen. Are you considering swimming across?"

Moses smiled with affection, his proper and shiny teeth that made him look more friendly appeared:

"Allah knows," he replied.

Sepi suddenly grew serious:

"We are ready to die with you."

The Red Sea was wilder than ever. The waves were gathering in the distance, growing as they got closer and rising like an eagle, then they would beat the shore one by one, one after the other. King Sepi happily said:

"Sinuha, Dear Friend, I have a surprise for you."

The treasurer turned his curious eyes to his friend. All of a sudden one of the shaky bodies hidden in covers behind Sepi moved slowly. When the covers were removed a beautiful woman body that seemed about thirty five years of age appeared. Sinuha's blue eyes opened in amazement. His heart started beating so wildly that he almost fainted.

"Tiye!" he yelled.

His voice was so loud that suddenly everyone looked at them.

His Tiye who he had suffered for and only dreamed of was standing right in front of him in white tulle. His head was spinning, he could hardly stand on his feet. His feelings were mixed, he couldn't say anything. Everything in his mind was gone, as if he had forgotten how to talk. He couldn't stop himself anymore. He hugged Tiye with love:

"Tiye, Dear Tiye. If flowers knew how deep my heart was hurt, they would cry with me to ease my pain. If nightingales knew how sad and ill I am they would sing sad songs. If the golden stars in the sky knew my pain, they would fall from the sky and murmur comforting words to me."

Tiye murmured in tears:

"Did you love me that much?"

"How could you know that I composed tiny melodies from the pain of separation, that I gave them jingling wings and sent them flying to you? However, unfortunately they weren't able to find the path to you. My dear Tiye, your green eyes made me forget all my pain."

* * *

As the Israelite tribes gathered on the shore of the Red Sea, bright lights appeared on the sand dunes on the horizon. The Pharaoh's army had swarmed on them just like a cloud of grasshoppers. Their swords and shields were turning into thousands of big and small mirrors with the scorching sun reflecting, along the shore sounds of the chariots, horses whinnying, and warriors' cries could be heard. With agility unexpected at his age Pharaoh Ramesses straightened up in his gold plated king's chariot. Raising his scepter, which was hooked at the end, to the sky, he stopped his army:

"O heroic army, as you can see the enemy consists of a handful of unarmed slaves. We have encircled them, there is nowhere they can escape, we shall wait for them to surrender."

The Pharaoh was afraid of war, he was hesitating about the revenge of Moses and his Lord.

Lamentation had begun in the Israelite tribes. Armed to the teeth and without mercy, the army of tyranny had followed them. They were all waiting to be slaughtered. Abel screamed in horror:

"We have been caught."

Their fear had reached maximum. Every minute they were getting closer to death, without any hope of being saved. From everywhere:

"We will be annihilated" screams were heard.

Prophet Moses got up on a high spot, and addressed his nation:

"We will not be annihilated, be patient."

"O Moses, the sea is ahead of us and the Pharaoh is behind us."

"Do not be afraid, our Lord is with us. He shall show us a way out."

Sinuha's voice was heard among the screaming:

"Where will we go O Moses?"

"Forward."

"But there is the sea there."

"My Lord doesn't lie, we will go forward."

Among the crowd Korah's high pitched voice was heard.

"We might as well be slaves to the Copts rather than drowning."

Samiri, who Moses had committed a murder for said:

"Did we come here to die under the swords of the Copts?"

Even though the Israelites were jabbering about Allah's Messenger they weren't attempting to leave him and take refuge in the Pharaoh. Their tyranny that had continued for years was forcing the Israelites to be with Moses. They couldn't forget the tortures that were done to them in dungeons, and they couldn't tolerate slavery. Their tongues, flesh and hands had been cut off, they had been tied to wheels.

* * *

The Prophet who felt that the Pharaoh was about to make a move ran towards the Red Sea, he was in water up to his knees. Suddenly he hit the water with his staff, and it was heard that he shouted:

"In the Name of Allah!"

Suddenly, something that amazed all living creatures happened. The Red Sea was splitting from the staff, among the water that had moved aside a wide road had opened. The salty water of the sea rose like mountains on both sides of the road. This was a view that nobody would have ever dreamed of. A dry road which they could cross over to the other side on had come about in front of them.

This was Divine salvation that abolished hopelessness and gave hope to the desperate. Without a second thought, the Israelites that witnessed the miracle began to proceed among the terrific walls of water. The road was wide enough for hundreds of people to walk side by side. The flood of people started to flow fast among the masses of water that rose like blue mountains on their both sides. They were moving so fast that half of them had already reached the other side. The Israelites had been tested to the last moment, but not a single one of them had asked for the Pharaoh's mercy.

With his small unit of soldiers, Sinuha had encircled Moses, and the last group which included the Prophets had started to walk slowly in the Red Sea. Not a single movement could be seen in the army of the Pharaoh.

Sinuha excitedly said:

"O Allah's Messenger, the Pharaoh is afraid of death."

The Prophet was busy thanking and praying to his Lord.

The Pharaoh and his army were horrified by this amazing scene. They were watching this supernatural event in amazement and confusion. Even though the last group was almost at the end of the road, the Pharaoh was hesitating to give the order to follow. Even though he was afraid and he wanted to return, his pride was stopping him from going back. His age had passed seventy five, but he had an agile body. Straightening up in his gold plated chariot with a grudge:

"Heroic soldiers, the Red Sea split with my power" he shouted.

His anger towards Allah's Messenger had driven him crazy. His heart was full of grudge and hatred. He gave his last order:

"Come on, kill until none of them are left alive."

As the Pharaoh drove his chariot to the sea, the group in which the Prophet was had reached the other shore. Suddenly hundreds of chariots and thousands of cavalry charged with battle cry. The Pharaoh had ordered his army to follow because he had seen the sea move to the sides and a wide road opening in the middle. With all its grandeur, the Egyptian army began to proceed along the dry road that the Israelites had just passed. The military units quickly entered between the walls of water rising on both sides of the road. When Prophet Moses shouted "In the Name of Allah" and hit the sea with his staff again the Pharaoh encountered a terrifying surprise. Something scary had happened all of a sudden, the walls of water that had separated a little while ago had rejoined all at once.

The road that the Israelites had safely passed a while ago had turned into a disaster for them, everything was swallowed by the water. Horses, chariots, soldiers, spears, swords and shields were all mixed up in the wild water. The screaming of people and the whinnying of horses were mixing, it was a life and death situation among the big waves of the sea.

Prophet Moses and thousands of believers of the Israelites had gathered on a high ground on the opposite shore, witnessing in curiosity mixed with fear, watching the invincible army of the Pharaoh disappearing among the waves in amazement. Moses spoke briefly:

"Nothing in the universe is abandoned or strayed. Nothing happens by itself as the heedless think. They rejected miracles, clear proof of the Lord, they claimed there was no returning to Allah, they rode the high horse in this world. See what becomes of tyrants. They are disappearing in the water like pebbles. The result of rebelling against Allah, revolting Him, is being wretched like this in both this world and the hereafter. This tragic ending is a great lesson for those who have a mind and consciousness. If our Lord wishes, He can annihilate deniers in an instant just like this. Let's pray that our Lord doesn't put us to hard tests, that He doesn't give us loads that we can't carry."

Abel whispered:

"When Moses was a helpless baby the water had been a refuge for him. The Pharaoh and his army entered the same water, but they perished. So, being safe is only possible by knowing Allah and believing in Him."

The Red Sea was full of dead bodies. There were nobles like Haman that had left all the benefactions they were enjoying life in, high flown commanders like Ubiante, Amon priests like Unas who was the only ruler of all temples. They had all pursued their benefits and egos, following the footsteps of the Pharaoh. Other than dead bodies, hundreds of horse carcasses, parts of chariots, saddles, harnesses, striped loincloths, sandals were floating on the water. Hundreds of chariots had sunk to the bottom of the sea at once.

* * *

The Israelites were delighted, they were celebrating by singing hymns altogether. Sinuha's loud voice rose among the crowd:

"Look, look at the water!"

He was pointing at an old person trying to swim. All eyes were locked on the blur in the water. This body fighting the waves was no one else but the tyrant and liar Pharaoh. There wasn't a sign of his usual strong and conceited look on his face that was bobbing in and out of the water. He was miserable and helpless, he was about to drown. As he rose above the water, with a weak voice:

"Save me" he was trying to shout out, asking for help.

He bobbed in and out a few times more, each time his voice was getting weaker. At that moment he was heard saying:

"I too believe in the God of Moses."

The answer of Allah's Messenger was meaningful:

"Are you believing now, when there is no other way for salvation? However you had always been arrogant, you recanted and denied."

Turning to his friends:

"Allah will prevent the decaying of the body of the Pharaoh who denied His miracles, so that the future generations can draw a lesson. Water will not break it up and fish will not eat it. For it not to be forgotten, his body will not rot."

Finally the Pharaoh disappeared in the wild waters of the Red Sea with his Nile blue crown and his closest men who he trusted so dearly.

* * *

After the Israelites watched the scary waves of the Red Sea, until there wasn't a single mark of the Pharaoh and his army left, drawing a lesson, they walked to brand new hopes led by their Prophet.

As Sinuha was disappearing in the distance towards Sinai with Tiye, he was gently singing these verses:

Nobody on earth or in the sky,

Is sad because of their perishing.

As an insect being exterminated,

They are fading away.

Those who held their heads high,

And trampled on people,

They are perishing, just like pests.

This universe that obeys its Lord.

Is happy to get rid of them.

Because as the whole universe believed in the Creator, they were denying.